WICKED BEAUTY

A WICKEDLY SPICY FAIRYTALE RETELLING

WICKED EVERMORE
BOOK ONE

INES JOHNSON

THOSE JOHNSON GIRLS

Cover Design by Fay Lane
Edited by Kasi Alexander

COASTAL KINGDOMS

FORBIDDEN FOREST
THORNHALL
GREYM
SNOW KINGDOMS
FENVALEN
VALEBRI
RAVENHOLD
TIDEHAVEN
INI
SEA KINGDOMS
E
EVERMORE

Cursed Realms
Beast Lands
...DOMS
...REST
Fire Islands

CHAPTER ONE

Mal stood at the edge of her garden, her dark eyes scanning the shadows for the disturbance that had dragged her from sleep. Something was wrong—something pressed on the horizon, in the direction of the castle. It pushed against her thoughts like a dream that refused to fade, or perhaps a nightmare with tendrils that clawed at her mind, desperate to take hold once in the waking hours.

She inhaled deeply. The heady scent of night-blooming jasmine filled her lungs. Its sweetness was overwhelming—cloying, almost suffocating. Beneath the saccharine aroma lay a sharp bitterness, faint but undeniable, leaving a trace of regret on her tongue.

Mal knelt, her claw-tipped fingers sinking into the rich earth. The fertile soil mirrored the color of her skin, deep and brown like the essence of life itself. The feel of the dirt grounded her, even as unease stirred within her chest.

A sound broke the stillness—a faint rustle. She lifted her gaze to the sight of a proud stag standing at the edge of the clearing. Its intricate antlers arched like the branches of an ancient oak, powerful and imposing, daring anything to challenge it. The stag's dark eyes locked with hers, its breath visible in the cool air between them.

Mal raised her head, the movement slow and deliberate. Her black horns curved upward in elegant spirals. As the full might of her presence became visible, the stag faltered. Its muscles twitched. Its hoof stamped once as tension rippled through the air. Then, with a sharp exhalation, it turned and cantered away, vanishing into the trees.

She watched it go, a frown tugging at her lips. Clearly the stag didn't know who she was, otherwise it wouldn't have run. It would have bowed low enough to the earth that its dark nose grazed her feet.

It took only three years for a deer to grow into its maturity. Three years for antlers like that to form. Three years for a stag's antlers to arch like the boughs of an ancient tree.

Had it been three years?

The forest beyond her small cottage stirred with life.

Trees groaned as they shifted in the evening breeze. Leaves unfurled, and night-blooming flowers opened their petals, whispering secrets to the stars. A sharp cry of prey falling to a predator's hunger echoed through the canopy before dissolving into the soft hum of night insects.

A new day was dawning. The sun's rays picked their way over Mal's roof before quickly moving on. Mal's home sat at the Enchanted Forest's border, deliberately removed from the cluster of cottages deeper within. Their roofs, thatched with moss and woven leaves, could be seen in the distance, clustered like a family huddled around a fire. Laughter drifted from that direction, faint but persistent—a reminder that others found solace in one another's company. Solace Mal had long since given up on.

Three years?

An elf and a sprite strolled along the forest path, their fingers entwined in affection. The tall, lithe elf carried themself with a graceful ease. Pastel eyeshadow adorned their lids, the soft hues catching the dappled sunlight filtering through the trees. Beside them, the smaller sprite walked with a confident, grounded stride. Their compact, muscular frame exuded a quiet strength. Their curving silhouette was balanced by delicate, shimmering wings, each flutter casting iridescent glimmers onto the mossy ground like fleeting stars.

Quiet laughter floated between them, light and intimate, carrying an air of unshakable trust and shared joy.

"Good morning, Guardian," trilled the sprite.

The elf's colorful brows rose at the sight of Mal. The elf shushed their love, putting themself between the sprite and Mal. "Beg pardon, Guardian."

Mal forced her expression into something cold and unmoved, as if it didn't matter. She'd perfected this—watching without wanting, listening without longing.

After all, she told herself, it was easier to be alone. Safer. Loneliness was predictable. You couldn't miss what you never let in. And Mal hadn't let anyone in for three years.

She watched the elf steer the sprite around an unsteady bit of earth. Once out of the path of danger, they pressed a kiss to the sprite's forehead. The gesture tried to stir up memories inside Mal. But it couldn't get past the jagged thing inside her to get at the memories she pretended she'd buried long ago.

The ache spread through her chest. Mal welcomed it. It was an old wound she'd learned to live with. The ache was proof that she was still standing. That the walls she'd built around herself hadn't crumbled—not yet.

Better to be alone, she reminded herself. Better to carry the ache of solitude than risk the agony of opening her heart again. His absence had taught her that. Love was a cruel teacher, and she wasn't eager to relearn the lesson.

It had been three years.

She had barely noticed a single day go by since she'd last seen him. She ran her hand along the rough bark of an oak tree, feeling the patterns beneath her fingertips. The forest reached out to her, asking for her guidance, for her leadership, for her protection. It was in the rustling of leaves, the faint glow of will-o'-the-wisps bobbing over the underbrush. But no matter how much magic lived within these woods, it couldn't fill the ache where his presence used to be.

A sharp *tap-tap* of wood on stone broke through the ambient noise. Mal didn't turn. She knew the steady rhythm of Doran's staff as well as she knew her own name. The elder dryad approached slowly. The weight of his expectations settled on her shoulders before he even spoke.

"You can't keep hiding here, Maleficent."

"You can see me. I'm not hiding."

Doran came closer, his ancient bark-skin crinkling as he studied her with quiet patience. "You are the Guardian of the Enchanted Forest. You weren't meant to live apart like this. The forest needs you."

"The forest is doing just fine without me."

"The forest is not fine. Ever since…"

Mal pressed her fingers to her temple. She saw Doran's mouth move, but his words were garbled. The collection of consonant and vowel sounds he made pricked at her mind like a needle. Of course they did. Anytime anyone said *his* name, it caused her heart, her head, her very being pain.

Then Doran said another name. A name full of soft vowels and rolling Rs that Mal heard quite clearly. That three-syllable collection of sounds pained her in an entirely different way.

"… It is your duty to Princess Aurora as the forest's representative."

Mal made a growling sound like the monster humans thought she was. Her lips curled, and her canines flashed as though she could taste the red blood of that snowy white princess on her tongue.

"The balance between humankind and forest folk is breaking, Maleficent. Your mother—"

"I am not my mother."

Unlike the stag or the sprites or fairies or even the humans of old, Doran was not afraid of her. He let the tempest of her words roll over him like a breeze through the leaves of his hair. "You are her daughter. Morwyn left Guardianship of the forests to you. As well as the flora, fauna, and folk who dwell here."

Mal opened her mouth to reply, to deny it, to damn

them all to hell—but a sudden flicker of movement caught her eye.

A youngling darted through the trees. The child didn't see that crumbling bit of ground the sprite and elf had skirted. It was hidden by roots and shadows, its edges slick from the recent rain. The child would fall, perhaps even fall through the cracks with that small, viny body of theirs. Without thinking, Mal moved.

She sprinted toward the child, her bare feet barely skimming the earth. Magic surged under her skin. She reached out with a flick of her wrist. Roots twisted and shot from the ground like serpents, weaving themselves into a net just as the youngling stumbled and fell.

The child let out a startled yelp as they tumbled into the cradle of roots. Mal skidded to her knees, pulling the child to safety just before the ground gave way beneath them.

Wide-eyed and trembling, the youngling clung to Mal, throwing small arms around Mal's neck in a desperate hug. The warmth of the child's embrace seeped into Mal. For a heartbeat, she hovered on the edge of something dangerous—connection.

Her hands flattened on the child's back. Her fingers settled and claws extended. Mal shoved the child away. "You need to be more careful."

"We were playing storm the castle." Though the

child was small, her voice was booming and bright. "I'm the princess."

"Learn this lesson well, child; no prince is coming to save you."

"Of course not," huffed the child, coming to stand on her own two feet. "I was coming to rescue the other princesses." She pointed to two small girls on the opposite side of the clearing. The young tykes had sharpened twigs in the belts over their tunics. "They're my friends. They would've come for me if I fell."

The child patted Mal's forearm as though to comfort her. Mal stood stiffly, brushing dirt from her hands as the youngling scurried away to rejoin her friends. The warmth of the child's embrace lingered on Mal's skin. She gave a shiver at the unwelcome sensation. The feeling clung stubbornly, like a ghost she couldn't shake.

From the corner of her eye, she saw Doran watching her. He said nothing. The look on his face was enough. He had seen everything—her instinct to protect, the spark of care she tried so hard to smother.

Without a word, Mal turned on her heel and strode back toward her cottage. The door slammed shut behind her. A sharp sting broke through her thoughts. She hissed softly and looked down at her hand.

There it was again—a scar. She had the vague memory of a needle pricking her fingertip some time ago. She'd wrapped the wound in a bandage, but it constantly throbbed as though a splinter were stuck there.

She rubbed at the spot absently, feeling the ache pulse from her fingertip all the way to her chest. The old wound never stopped hurting. It was a constant reminder of everything she'd lost. Though now the pain felt sharper, more immediate—like the universe itself was driving the point deeper into her soul. Like the dream that woke her and brought her to the door was looming over her, ready to turn dark.

Mal's hand drifted to her chest. Her fingers curled over the hollow ache she pretended didn't exist. It had been three years since she lost Phillip. Three years since she had let anyone get close enough to matter. And for three years, she had told herself that loneliness was better than loss. But for the briefest of moments, when she'd held the child in her arms, she hadn't felt lonely.

And that scared her more than anything.

CHAPTER TWO

*P*hillip rubbed absently at the scar on his fingertip, the rough patch of skin catching beneath the calluses on his thumb. It was a small thing —barely visible, really—but the ache it left behind lingered, stubborn and persistent. He traced it with his index finger as if by doing so, he might unlock the memory of how it came to be.

He had no memory of pricking his finger, yet there it was. A thin, pale line that had been with him for years. Two? Maybe three years, refusing to heal. Once, out of sheer frustration, he'd gone to see a healer. They'd squinted at the scar, poking at it with mild curiosity before dismissing it as some phantom pain or minor irritation.

This morning, the ache was sharper than usual, as

though the scar had a mind of its own. A soft breeze rolled through the open balcony doors, carrying the faint, bittersweet aroma of jasmine. He paused, his hand lowering to his side. The scent tugged at him, stirring something restless and hollow in his chest. It was so familiar—so achingly familiar. Jasmine, tinged with a faint bitterness, like a memory just out of reach.

It reminded him of the forests, of running wild amidst the trees, of *her*.

That smell was the first thing that made it feel like home when he'd returned to the castle in the dead of night after three years of war at the borderlands with the trolls. The small regiment that accompanied him had cheered their return, relishing the prospect of hot meals and warm beds. Phillip had found no comfort. Not in the stone walls, the tapestries, or even the gardens. Nothing had felt like home—not without her.

Phillip rolled his neck, hearing the tendons crack and protest at the movement. He'd had a restless night of sleep, as he had every night since losing her. The bed was too soft, the air too still, his thoughts too loud. He'd thrown himself into the war at the borderlands, desperate to make something hurt the way he did. The trolls had fallen; the border was safe, and his people had hailed him a hero. The victory rang hollow.

Instead of a daylight parade, he'd returned to the castle under the cover of darkness, hoping that the familiarity of his rooms might grant him some measure of peace. But nothing felt the same. The scent of her was gone from his pillows, replaced by the faint, clean fragrance of lavender sachets left by the maids.

Now in the pale morning light, he gazed at the tangled green outside his window, the ache in his chest as stubborn as the scar on his finger. He reached out, tracing the jagged lines of the vine nearest to him, the cool dew clinging to his fingertips. The vines she had once used to climb into his chambers at night were overgrown with disuse, curling around the stone walls in wild tangles.

He exhaled slowly, feeling the familiar exhaustion settle over him like a heavy cloak. He was always tired these days, dragging himself through the hours of his life as if he carried an invisible burden. The only time the exhaustion lifted was when he actually slept.

Because in his dreams, she was waiting for him.

He closed his eyes, and there she was. Her skin was the color of rich earth, warm and grounding. Her lips, full and deep red, needed no beauty paint to draw his attention. Her dark eyes, rimmed in kohl, held the secrets of the forests, endless and knowing, as if they saw straight through him. And those horns—twisting and spiraling upward like an ancient crown—had fascinated him since childhood.

He remembered the first time she had let him touch

them. He'd been a boy then, filled with curiosity and reverence, even though he was the one with the royal title. She had leaned her head toward him with a mischievous smile. His fingers had brushed the smooth curve of her horns. The sound she made—a low, contented sigh—had sent a strange warmth curling through his chest. He had spent the rest of that day grinning like a fool, though he'd never quite understood why.

Years later, she'd let him touch them again. This time the sigh had been a deep moan of pleasure. That night, he'd not only touched her horns, he'd tasted them. Then he'd tasted every part of her, leaving her gasping in ecstasy.

Phillip's hand tightened on the brick of the balcony as the memory washed over him. Dreams were all he had of her now. The woman he could no longer hold. She had vanished from his life, like smoke slipping through his fingers.

"Phillip?" A voice cut through the quiet. "Phillip, darling, are you sleeping?"

"No, I'm up, Rory. I'll be out in a—"

She didn't wait for permission to enter. Aurora stepped inside, her golden hair catching the low light like spun silk, her gown trailing behind her in delicate waves.

Aurora moved with the grace of someone who

believed she belonged wherever she stood, including Phillip's most private spaces. She did belong, of course—she was his bride-to-be. The wedding arrangements had been made long ago when they were children, a union for the good of the kingdom, a duty Phillip never questioned. At least not as a child. It was simply what was expected of him: learn to fight, take the crown, marry the princess, rule the lands.

That was the agenda of his life. What was not on the agenda was admitting Aurora into his heart. She had been promised his hand, but someone else had stolen that organ.

Aurora was a great friend and an excellent monarchial partner. She'd managed the day-to-day minutia of the kingdom while he'd been out fighting. Her beauty should have stirred him. Her kindness should have softened him. Phillip had never felt the pull to invite her into his bed.

"Good, you're awake." She brushed a strand of hair behind her ear and perched lightly on the edge of a nearby chair, her hands folded neatly in her lap. "You're needed at court. Something to do with the expansion."

The great expansion had been his father's vision, along with the last Forest Guardian. Before he and Morwyn could bring their vision to life, the trolls had attacked. His father had been taken at the start of the troll wars. Morwyn had fought at the old king's side.

Now the war was won and Phillip was the only one left with the vision. Though he supposed that wasn't true. Someone had to have replaced Mal in the years he'd been gone. He'd likely be meeting that person today, as the Forest Guardian had a chair on the council. Once again, that spot on his finger prickled.

"I've been gone for three years, Aurora. You've done an excellent job leading the council. I'm certain you don't need me stepping in."

His words were true. He'd seen the improvements within the castle walls when he'd arrived last night—the levy system, the water control measures. It was impressive work. He couldn't wait to see what had been done in the forests.

"The forest folk are not honoring your father's original vision for unity and growth. They're... resistant to progress."

"Resistant?"

In his mind, he saw the forest—not as a wilderness to be tamed but as a home. A place alive with magic, the place where Mal had once belonged. He saw her as she had been, fierce and vibrant, her horns spiraling upward like crowns of twisted wood, her smile unguarded while rare. That smile had always made him feel like he belonged, like the forest itself accepted him because she did.

He rubbed the scar again. The ache in his chest was

sharper than the one in his hand. Maybe it was foolish, but he wanted to believe that what he was doing now, what he was building with Aurora, could honor Mal's memory.

Phillip hadn't considered that his absence might cause tension or delay after the expansion. When he'd gone to fight, it was because—well, yes, because of his anger over the loss of the woman he loved. But it was also because he believed in the union of Folkind and Humankind. It pained him to know that divisions were once again coming between the two people.

"I'll be right down."

Aurora rose as though gliding on a soft cloud. She smiled up at him as though he'd hung the moon and gave his forearm a squeeze. And then she was gone.

Her scent lingered—warm lavender. It mingled with the hint of jasmine coming through the windows. The two scents clashed, just as Aurora and Mal had often clashed.

Phillip had hoped that the two women in his life would eventually become friends. That one day they might find common ground in their duty to their people. That, perhaps, they might set aside their differences for his sake. Being caught in the middle of two fierce women might be a fantasy for weaker men. It had been a harsh reality for Prince Phillip.

Mal had his heart, always had, from the first

moment he'd seen her walking barefoot through the woods, her black horns catching the sunlight. She was the girl he had fallen in love with, the one who had shown him the beauty of the forests and the magic within them.

Aurora had his hand. She was the one he was bound to by duty and expectation. The one his mother had chosen for him to wed. He had been raised to believe that duty was the cornerstone of his life.

His father's voice echoed in his mind, stern and unwavering: "A king does what is required of him, even at the cost of his own happiness."

It had never once occurred to Phillip that anything intimate would ever happen between him and Aurora. His heart would not allow it. It belonged wholly to Mal in a way he could never have given to anyone else. He also never seriously considered not marrying Aurora. The idea of abandoning the expectations of his crown, his people, had always seemed... impossible.

And yet, for some reason, the two women refused even to consider friendship, much less cordiality. Aurora had viewed Mal with suspicion from the start, as if her very presence were a challenge to her position. And Mal—Mal had barely disguised her disdain for Aurora, dismissing her as little more than a pawn in someone else's game.

Phillip inhaled. His nostrils were hit with the

clashing scents of lavender and jasmine—sweet, bitter, and impossible to reconcile. But he had no choice.

All he had left was Aurora. Her friendship had gotten him through the worst of Mal's loss. Mal would likely scowl at that. He would give anything to see that beautiful frown.

He rubbed his scar one last time, wishing the pain would reveal something—anything—about the night he'd lost her. Wishing that the dreams wouldn't dissolve each morning, leaving only the faintest trace of her touch.

CHAPTER THREE

*M*al's steps were silent on the mossy ground of the forest. The trees bent toward her as she passed. Their branches swayed in reverence. Leaves brushed gently against her shoulders like silent bows. Wildflowers bloomed brighter at her feet, petals unfurling to catch her gaze. Vines curled upward in a slow, elegant dance, beckoning for her attention. Creatures peeked from burrows and tree-tops, their eyes glinting with admiration.

She ignored them all.

Once, she might have felt comforted by the forest's love for her, the way the green space pulsed with life at her presence. Once, she had welcomed it, accepted the crown it offered. Not a crown of gold, but of roots and leaves, of magic intertwined with responsibility.

That was before. Before the weight of expectation had crushed her spirit. Before the world took too much from her.

She was not a Guardian, like her mother before her, and her mother before her on back since the first Folkind punched through the earth to breathe the air. She was not a queen, nor a protector. She was tired. Tired of the forest's love, tired of the responsibility that came with it. She had lost her mother to duty. Lost Phillip to fate. What was left of her heart wasn't enough to give to anything or anyone, not even the land that still whispered her name with every breeze.

The path to the edge of the forest wound through ancient trees, their gnarled roots tangled like old hands clutching secrets. Mal didn't need a clear path. She knew the way without looking. Her feet stepped one in front of the other out of habit.

At last, she reached the clearing where the ring of sacred trees stood. They were towering oaks, older than kingdoms, their branches wide enough to touch the sky. Here, at the border between the human world and the forest's ancient heart, she had met Phillip countless times. As children, when they built forts of sticks and leaves. As teenagers, when their laughter echoed through the glade. And later, as lovers, when the silence between them was filled with weighted sighs and unspoken promises.

Mal's gaze was fixed on the stump near the end of the tree ring. The roots beneath it, once mighty and sprawling, now lay dormant, entwined with the labyrinth of the earth. It had not been cut down. No axe had severed its life. One day the tree had pulled up its roots, coalesced its branches into strong arms, and formed its leaves into a head. That tree had left its immortality and formed itself into a man because it had fallen in love with the last Guardian.

"Hello, Father."

Her fingers brushed the rough bark, her claw-tipped nails tracing the grooves of what was left. The stump stood like a sentinel, a reminder of what had been given up for love. Once, her father had stood among these trees, his roots deep in the earth, his branches reaching for the heavens. He had been as eternal as the forest itself, a being of endless wisdom and strength. That had changed the day Morwyn stepped over his roots and his heart had tripped.

Eredan had loved her mother, a fae who had stolen his heart with her laughter and her fierce devotion to the forest. Together, they had lived as Guardians of the forest. But love had its cost. His life, once endless, had been shortened. He had withered after a few hundred years, his body returning to the soil he had once nurtured.

Morwyn had nearly followed him into the earth.

Her grief had been a shadow that lingered, a weight that threatened to pull her down. But she had stayed, teaching Mal everything she needed to know to become the next Guardian. Only when her task was complete had she joined her love in the soil, their roots entwined for eternity.

Mal's hand drifted over the bark, tracing the smooth lines where two names had been carved. The letters shimmered faintly with magic. She remembered the day they had made those marks, the way Phillip had asked her father for permission, his voice soft and reverent. The bark had accepted their love, parting willingly to cradle the letters they carved—an eternal symbol of their union.

She felt Phillip's presence, distant but tangible, like the warmth of a sunbeam hidden by a cloudy day. He was gone. But here, in this place, he was still with her. A part of her longed to stay, to sink into the memories and pretend that the world beyond the glade did not exist. Just as she let her eyes drift closed, the smell of something foul met her nostrils. The sound of a crash shattered the quiet.

In the distance, trees toppled like dominoes, their trunks splintering with sickening cracks. Massive metal machines rumbled through the forest, their gears grinding and engines roaring, belching smoke into the air. The acrid tang of iron assaulted Mal's senses. The bitter scent clawed at her nose. The ground trembled beneath her feet as ancient trees fell one by one, their leaves scattering like lost souls, fleeing the destruction wrought upon their sanctuary.

She shot to her feet. Adrenaline surged through her veins. The forest that had nurtured her, that still whispered her name, was being torn apart—its roots ripped from the earth, its magic bleeding into the soil. The forest's cries resonated in her chest. This wasn't just an attack on the trees or the land—it was a desecration of everything her parents had fought to protect. A low growl built in her throat. The roots beneath her feet quivered in response, awaiting her command.

The machines bulldozed forward, crushing everything in their path with merciless efficiency. Mal sprinted toward the destruction, her boots pounding against the forest floor. Vines and branches shifted out of her way, eager to aid her, sensing the fire that had reignited in her soul.

"Stop!" she shouted. Her voice was swallowed by the roar of the machines.

The forest's pain, its desperation, felt as if it were her own. The ache in her chest sharpened into resolve, and for the first time in years, she let herself feel the weight of responsibility. But as she neared the edge of the clearing, the acrid tang of iron grew stronger, stinging her senses.

She stopped short, her breath hitching. The machines were coated in it—thick, gleaming layers of iron on their gears and blades, designed to repel magic like hers. The material was a venomous hum, even from a distance, a barrier that made her magic flicker and falter like a flame against a strong wind.

She was fae, but the forest was earth. Millions of years ago, the flora had grown around the metal ores deep in Evermore's core. It would do the same today.

With a flick of her wrist, she called on the roots beneath the ground, commanding them to rise. They shot from the earth like serpents, thick and twisting, wrapping around the wheels of the bulldozers, halting their advance. The machines groaned and sputtered, gears grinding uselessly as the forest fought back.

Mal planted herself in front of the fallen trees, her breath ragged, her magic thrumming through every nerve. She stood at the edge of the forest she had once abandoned, facing the destruction head-on.

She had lost too much already. She would not lose another inch.

The scent of smoke stung her nose. The char of bark turned her stomach. The vibrations of the machines rumbled as the earth swallowed them, sinking the behemoths into the ground.

The men shouted in confusion, scrambling out of the vehicles before they were eaten, too. Their swords hissed free from their scabbards, steel gleaming in the fading light. They fanned out, surrounding Mal. Mal rolled her eyes at the display. And then she rolled her head around her neck, letting loose the tendons and tension that had been building up for years.

The men lunged, blades flashing. Mal moved with the fluid grace of a dancer, her body twisting as she sidestepped the first strike. She caught the man's wrist mid-swing, twisting it until the sword clattered to the ground. With a quick flick of her hand, a vine shot up and coiled around his legs, dragging him backward into the underbrush.

Another soldier charged, sword raised high. Mal met him head-on, her horns lowering in defense. The curved tips caught his armor with a metallic scrape, throwing him off balance. She shoved him backward with her shoulder, and he stumbled, landing hard on his back.

She spread her arms, and the forest responded. Branches reached out like arms. Roots snaked along the ground. Vines lashed toward the soldiers, dragging them down one by one.

The last man standing gritted his teeth, fear flickering in his eyes. He gripped his sword with shaking hands but didn't swing. "We—we were under orders."

Mal stepped closer, her green eyes glowing bright with malice. "Whose orders?"

He swallowed hard, stumbling over his words. To Mal, it sounded like a jumble of names, muffled and meaningless—until one name rang clear.

"Aurora."

CHAPTER FOUR

$\mathcal{P}$hillip sat at the long council table. His fingers rested lightly on the wooden surface. It looked like oak, though he knew it wasn't. Oaks were sacred in this region—sacred and sentient. The material was likely pine. That species had never evolved into awareness. Though Phillip had his doubts after being bonked on the head by more than one pinecone in his life.

He traced the grain of the wood as the voices around him droned on. The midday sun filtered through narrow windows, casting stripes of light across the room. Even in the warm glow, Phillip felt a strange chill settle in his chest. His scar throbbed again, sharp and insistent.

"We've had some... resistance from the fae folk in

the Enchanted Forests," one of the councilmen said, his tone dismissive.

Phillip barely knew the man. Lord Queros. He had been an assistant to Lord Rowanthor before Phillip left for the borderlands. Now Queros held the man's seat. In fact, many of the seats were occupied by younger lords. Not a single lady. Not a single fae.

"Why isn't the Forest Guardian in attendance at this meeting?"

The room went silent. All heads turned toward Phillip. Lord Queros opened and closed his mouth like a fish that had been pulled out of water.

"They were invited," Aurora piped in, her voice trilling with diplomacy. "However, they have never once shown up in the three years you've been away."

"Attendance from fairies," Queros sneered. "They're little more than relics of a bygone era. An evolutionary misstep before humankind rose to dominance."

Phillip's hand curled into a fist beneath the table. Was this the way the entire table thought? No wonder the current Guardian didn't bother making an appearance. That would stop today.

Before Phillip could respond, Aurora's voice rang out. Not raised. Rory never raised her voice. Nevertheless, her tone came out smooth and commanding. "That is enough."

The councilman closed his fish-mouth. Around him,

every gaze shifted toward the princess. Aurora sat beside Phillip, serene and poised, her golden hair catching the light like a crown. She folded her hands in her lap, her expression calm but unyielding.

"The fae were here long before we built our kingdoms. And though the fairy godmothers no longer answer our calls, it is still our responsibility to maintain peace. The human population is growing. Our advancements are outpacing what magic has done for this realm. If we are to thrive, we must move forward—but carefully."

Her words were measured. Her tone was thoughtful. The councilmen bowed their heads in silent agreement. Phillip watched them closely, noting the way even the most arrogant among them seemed subdued in the face of her reasoning. He felt a flicker of gratitude toward Aurora. She always knew what to say, how to navigate contrary people with grace and precision.

Not for the first time, he wished he could love her the way he'd once loved Mal. The way he still did love Mal. At some point over the last three years, his heartbeat had quieted, almost as though it slumbered. These days, his heart barely beat at all. It was sluggish, weighed down by grief, dragging through every moment like a heavy stone.

Another report was handed across the table. Phillip scanned the parchment, and his pulse quickened.

"The machines are moving too close to the border. That area there —" He pointed to the spot on the map where the ring of sacred trees stood. "That area is... significant. It should remain untouched."

Before anyone could respond, a distant commotion echoed through the hallways. The sounds of voices raised, feet stomping, and hurried movement reached inside the closed council room doors. The noise was muffled, the words garbled as if spoken through water.

Phillip frowned, turning his head toward the door, straining to hear. Aurora touched his arm, snagging his attention away from whatever was happening outside.

"I know you have an affinity for the fae folk. Why don't you take this map and cordon off the areas you wish to protect?"

The commotion sounded louder. It tugged at Phillip's attention with urgency. Aurora's fingers were gentle on his cheek as she turned his attention back to her.

"The sooner you go, the sooner you can ensure nothing sacred is disturbed."

She was right. The last thing he wanted was for that particular part of the forest to see any disquiet. But another part of him wanted to see to the shouting. It felt... important.

"Trust me. I'll take care of the rest."

Aurora's voice was soothing, like a lullaby. The

unease in Phillip's chest loosened. The tension in his shoulders dissipated under her calm gaze. She always knew what needed to be done. She always had a plan.

"I'll see to it," he said.

Aurora's smile deepened as he rose from his seat at the table. Phillip felt himself sink into the comfort of her assurance. She would handle things. She always did.

As he left the chamber, the ache in his fingertip flared again, sharp as a needle. He ignored it. The sacred tree was near the boundary. If he could just get there in time, he could protect it.

Mounting his horse, Phillip adjusted his grip on the reins. His leather gloves creaked faintly against the worn straps. He nudged his steed, and it cantered out of the stables and onto the cobbled streets.

Once a bustling hub of activity with open gates and merchants hawking their wares, the castle grounds now felt... constrained. The gates that had stood wide during his childhood were shut tight. The thick bars were a symbol of security but also a grim reminder of isolation. The walls loomed higher than he remembered, freshly reinforced, casting long shadows over the cobbled streets. Guards patrolled the perimeter with mechanical precision, their armor clinking as they moved.

The people milling about the courtyard seemed weary. Children played near the fountain, their laughter subdued, while mothers watched with furrowed brows. Farmers unloaded sacks of grain under the watchful eyes of overseers, their movements brisk, almost anxious. The levy system was impressive, true, and the walls impenetrable, but they had turned the castle into a fortress rather than a home.

Was this what the war had brought? Peace bound so tightly by fear that it strangled joy?

The thought left him once the gates were opened and the wide expanse of the forest was on the horizon. The forest had always been his escape back then— open, wild, and free. With a flick of his wrist and a gentle squeeze of his thighs, he spurred his horse into a gallop. The wind whipped against his face as he rode toward the forest. His cape billowed behind him. When he got to the edge of the forest, he saw it was too late.

The growl of engines was gone, leaving only the murmur of restless men clustered near their now-stalled machines. Phillip dismounted from his steed and tethered it to one of the trees that had fallen. The men straightened as they saw him approach.

"What happened here?"

A broad-shouldered soldier with dirt smeared across his face stepped forward, wiping his hands on his trousers. "A fairy stopped us, Your Highness."

The man sounded like he had a mouthful of

marbles. The ache in Phillip's scarred fingertip deepened. "A fairy?"

"Yeah," another man chimed in, though his voice carried the same strange distortion. "She came outta nowhere—stopped the machines dead with flowers and sticks."

The scar was hot beneath Phillip's glove. Something stirred in the back of his mind, a memory just out of reach. Something sharp, like a needle. But it slipped away before he could grasp the full picture.

"Listen to me carefully," Phillip said. "You are not to cross this boundary again. This part of the forest is off-limits."

The men shifted uncomfortably. One of them, braver than the others, muttered, "But Princess Aurora gave us the orders."

That was clearly a lie. Phillip would have this man's job for it. His tongue, too, if he spread more falsehoods about Rory. Or perhaps it hadn't been Aurora at all. He could see Lord Queros giving the order in Aurora's name.

"I am your prince. Soon I will be king. My word will stand above all others. Do you understand?"

The men exchanged uneasy glances but nodded. "Yes, Your Highness."

Phillip gave them a curt nod and turned toward the forest. The tension in his chest eased somewhat as he led his horse over the fallen trees and raised roots. When he approached the sacred tree ring, the air grew thick with memories that clung to the place like mist. The bark of Eredan's stump shimmered faintly, old magic woven into its ancient fibers. Phillip's boots crunched softly on the fallen leaves as he stepped closer, tracing his gloved fingers along the letters carved into the wood. The scar on his fingertip burned hotter, and for a moment, he swore he could feel her—Mal.

"Welcome back, Your Highness."

Doran emerged from the shadows, his staff tapping lightly against the ground with each step. His bark-like skin gleamed in the dim light filtering through the trees. A small, knowing smile curved his lips.

Phillip rose to embrace the old dryad. "It has been a long time, hasn't it?"

"Too long." Doran's old eyes sparkled with something that made Phillip's chest tighten—a sense of belonging, of familiarity, as if the forest itself welcomed him back after his absence.

Phillip ran a hand through his hair, suddenly weary. "I'm sorry about how far they got before I interfered."

"Many things are happening in the forest. Things that were set in motion long before you or I arrived on this mossy rock."

Phillip wanted to talk to the dryad about Mal. He

ached for a memory of his love that Doran might have tucked away. A story from one of the few days that they were apart after their first introduction. Anything. But her name wouldn't leave his lips.

"Ah. It seems some curses burrow deeper than the oldest roots," Doran said, tilting his head with a thoughtful expression.

"Curse?"

Doran gave him that tree-wizened look, the kind that hinted at answers Phillip wasn't ready to hear.

"Come," Doran said, gesturing toward the village beyond the tree. "Now that you've returned, let us not waste what time we have."

CHAPTER FIVE

"S top right there!"

Mal ignored the command and continued on through the castle gates. Her boots slammed against the stone floor, each step echoing with purpose. Clanging swords and armor announced the guards' approach as they rushed to block her path. Mal didn't slow.

Magic thrummed beneath her skin. She felt the live elements of the earth beneath her feet like a storm on the verge of quaking the castle's foundations. With a flick of her wrist, she summoned the forest to her aid. Vines erupted from the ground, slithering through cracks in the stone walls, wrapping around the guards' legs and pulling them off balance. Decaying flowers sprang back to life and stems unfurled, their crinkling petals puffing ashen pollen into the air.

The guards staggered, coughing and sneezing as the plants' spores overwhelmed them. One by one, their weapons clattered to the ground, useless at their feet.

Mal didn't spare them a second glance. She marched forward, her heart pounding in her chest like a war drum. She rounded a corner and spotted her.

Aurora.

The princess sat at the far end of the table in the council's chambers. Mal knew this room well. She'd been here many times as her mother and the old king had their discussions. She and Phillip would play under the tables, telling each other tales. When they were older, they sat side by side with Phillip whispering in her ear of the depraved things he would do to her once he got her alone.

Aurora sat in the spot that Mal had once occupied. Phillip's seat was empty.

More guards appeared behind her. Their swords were drawn. They blocked her way out. Mal had no intention of leaving until she had spoken her piece… or preferably punched the princess in her pretty pert nose.

Vines twisted beneath her skin, eager to be unleashed, to coil around these men and cast them aside like fallen leaves. Before she could summon them, Aurora's voice drifted through the air—soft and sweet, like the petals of a rose hiding a venomous thorn.

"Let her pass."

The guards hesitated, glancing between Mal and their princess. Aurora's sweet smile was all kindly reassurance. Slowly, reluctantly, the guards lowered their weapons. They kept them pointed in Mal's direction, as if they believed her to be as dangerous as a wildfire.

Mal ignored them. Her gaze locked on Aurora. She moved forward like a predator, her pulse hammering in her ears as she cornered her prey.

The council members, who had been gathered in quiet murmurs around the large table, froze as the tension thickened in the room. Their eyes darted between the poised guards and the dark figure of Maleficent. As if a silent signal passed among them, they began to scurry out like frightened mice abandoning a burning barn.

Robes rustled, chairs scraped against the stone floor, and the metallic clink of a dropped quill echoed briefly before someone kicked it aside in their haste to get out. One council member, an older man with a trembling hand, cast a nervous glance over his shoulder as Mal's horns caught the dim light of the room. His lips moved as if in silent prayer before he followed the others out. By the time the doors shut behind the last of them, the room was empty save for the guards, Aurora, and Mal.

There she was—her nemesis. Just as beautiful as the day Phillip had introduced them as children. Aurora's skin gleamed like polished porcelain. Her eyes were the pale blue of a morning sky. Golden hair framed her face in perfect waves. Her lips curved into a smile so demure it could have belonged to a saint. She looked like a dream, a vision crafted from sunlight and silk.

Mal had seen past that façade the moment they'd met. Aurora was no fresh bloom—she was a poison. The kind of flower that sprouted bright and lovely, its scent intoxicating, lulling folk into a false sense of safety. But beneath those petals lay a deadly toxin, waiting for the right moment to seep into the veins of the unsuspecting and stop their heart. The royal damsel was all polished surface, concealing the rot within.

"You've finally decided to show up and do your duty, Guardian."

Mal stepped closer, closing the distance until only a breath of air separated them. Her magic simmered just beneath her skin, ready to lash out the moment Aurora made a move. The scent of lavender lingered in the air between them—Aurora's perfume, as soft and cloying as her voice. It reminded Mal of something Phillip had once said about Aurora, that she smelled like spring. At the time, Mal had laughed bitterly, thinking how fitting it was that something so lovely could also be so fleeting and dangerous.

"Why are you doing this?"

"What am I doing, dear?"

As soon as Mal asked her question, she realized she didn't care about Aurora's answer. What made the rage inside her go from simmer to boil was the use of that word. The others would hear the polite princess use an endearment. Mal knew that Aurora called her deer as an insult.

"I'm doing what Phillip wanted. He wanted peace between our kinds. He bade me to protect the forest before he…" And there she trailed off, her fingers fluttering through the air along with the unfinished sentence.

But that was just it. Mal didn't know what had happened to Phillip. One day he was there, and the next day he wasn't.

"*I* am ensuring Phillip's wishes are followed." Aurora pressed a dainty hand to the place on her chest where a heart should lie. Mal swore she heard a thump echo from the empty cavern.

"By tearing up the forests he loved?"

"Oh, yes, I heard there was a misstep at the boundary this morning. You could've warned us ahead of time had you attended any of the council meetings over the years. Since you hadn't, we had to make our best guesses about the stumps."

Blades clanged up and made a clashing sound inches

from her neck. It wasn't the threat of her blood spilling that had Mal backing down. It was the tang of iron weakening her power.

Her gaze flicked down to Aurora's hand, where a familiar ring gleamed on her finger—Phillip's engagement ring. The sight of it twisted something deep inside Mal.

Why was Aurora still wearing it? Likely only to bait Mal.

"I've already lost Phillip. Why must you try to take my home, too?"

Aurora lifted her hand as though admiring the ring, turning it slowly in the light. Her eyes glittered, but her smile stayed soft, sweet—so saccharine it made Mal's skin crawl. "Phillip chose his duty. He always did. He was never yours to keep."

"He would never have married you if he had a choice," Mal hissed. "You were nothing but duty to him."

"Believe what you want, deer. But I am doing what Phillip wanted. What you both wanted. Humans will live in the forests, and the forest folk will be welcomed in the cities. Humans need labor, after all. Domestic help. Someone to tend the floors and take the trash out."

And with that, Aurora made a shooing motion to the guards. They clamped their iron-gloved hands on Mal's forearms and shoved her bodily toward the door.

Magic unfurled from her hands in shimmering tendrils of green and gold. But just as the magic rose, a sharp cramp shot through her hand, seizing the flesh where the tiny prick of her scar still lingered. Mal hissed in pain, flexing her fingers, trying to force the cramp away.

Aurora's eyes gleamed with a devilish glint, as though she knew exactly what Mal was feeling. She stepped closer, leaning in until her breath brushed against Mal's ear, her voice a low murmur meant only for Mal.

"There's nothing you can do to stop me. Go home, Maleficent. Pull up the weeds. Make it nice and pretty for your new mistress."

Aurora straightened, her expression serene, as though she hadn't just planted venom in Mal's heart. Then, without another word, she turned and walked away, her gown swaying gracefully behind her.

She didn't look back. She didn't need to. The message was clear—that damsel wasn't the prey. Mal wasn't cornered. She was summarily tossed out of the castle on her ass.

CHAPTER SIX

$\mathcal{A}$ breeze stirred the leaves overhead, carrying with it the faintest trace of wildflowers and the memory of rain. Phillip moved deeper into the forest, his boots whispering against the moss-covered ground. He'd left his horse at a stable at the top of the main road into the forests. Had he brought his steed any deeper, both the fauna and the horse would have spooked one another.

As he walked, the forest hummed with life. Everywhere he looked, memories flickered like ghosts just beyond his reach. He saw himself as a child, running through these woods, chasing after Mal as her laughter rose to the treetops. He could still see the way the light danced in her eyes, the way her horns gleamed when the sun kissed them just right. He remembered the feel of her hand in his—strong, warm, and always a little rough from her magic.

He brushed past a familiar tree. A flicker of their younger selves sitting together beneath its branches went through his mind. Mal's voice, smoky and teasing, drifted on the wind. Phillip closed his eyes and let himself feel her fingers threading through his as they went on one of their adventures.

Gods, he missed her.

A rustle in the underbrush pulled him from the memory. He opened his eyes to find several forest folk emerging from the shadows—sprites, dryads, and fae. Their eyes were wary. A few faces were twisted in anger. A few others held postures that were tense and ready to strike.

"You finally found the courage to show your face here, prince of men?" one of them demanded, his voice sharp and bitter. "Why are you destroying our homes? We thought you were on our side."

Phillip held his hands up in a gesture of peace. "I'm sorry for the destruction of the machines. I've already cleared up the misunderstanding. There will be no more bulldozing. You have my word."

The forest folk murmured among themselves, exchanging uneasy glances.

Phillip stepped closer.

"I've been away for too long. I left to fight off the

trolls and ogres who were threatening the borderlands. Now our borders are safe, but I see that my absence at home caused harm. For that, I'm truly sorry. I will make this right."

The murmurs softened, but the tension in the air remained. It buzzed like the wings of the sprites hovering near the treetops. Some shifted uneasily, their gossamer wings twitching, while others stood with arms crossed, casting furtive glances behind him as if waiting for something—or someone.

Phillip caught the faintest motion out of the corner of his eye. Vines curled and uncurled along the ground. The movement sent a chill up his spine. He'd seen this before—long ago, when the forest answered the call of its Guardian.

Two warrior fae emerged from the shadows, their stance firm and commanding. Yet their movements were fluid, precise, almost as though they were being guided.

Memories rushed back—of a time when Mal's mother had walked these very paths, the forest alive with her presence. The reverence the fae folk showed now was the same as it had been then, an unspoken acknowledgment of a power greater than any of them.

The vines writhed again, snaking along the ground toward him. He scanned the shadows but saw nothing save for the warriors with their heads bent toward an empty space as though they were conferring with it. The empty space rippled and shimmered like there was a presence there.

Was it the new Guardian? He strained to see, but there was no figure stepping into the light. No one revealed themselves. Only the forest pulsing with power. He knew something was there in the nothingness because all eyes were on it.

Doran tapped his staff lightly against the mossy ground. The sound was rhythmic, steady—a heartbeat in the tense silence.

"Doran, what is it? Who are they talking to?"

The dryad tilted his head, studying Phillip closely. "You can't see her, can you?"

"See who?"

Doran said nothing, and in the dryad's silence, Phillip heard it. The unmistakable echo of her voice drifted through the air. It was faint, like the memory of a dream. It set his pulse racing as though his heart were trying to break free from his chest and run to her. The scent followed—a wild, untamed fragrance that was uniquely hers. It wasn't jasmine or anything cultivated; it was the scent of earth after rain, the freshness of untouched forests, and the faint sweetness of night-blooming flowers.

Phillip's hand lifted without his permission, reaching toward the space the others were focused on.

At first, he felt nothing—just air, cool and empty. He reached again. This time, his fingertips brushed against something solid.

Warm. Familiar.

His hand found skin. Smooth. Radiant.

His fingers curled slightly, afraid the sensation would vanish if he let go.

A surge of energy shot through him, starting at his fingertips and racing up his arm, setting every nerve on edge. He was on the edge of something big, something bright. It felt like waking from the deepest sleep. It was like a shroud that had smothered him for years was suddenly being torn away. His heart, sluggish and heavy for so long, kicked into overdrive, pounding against his ribs with a rapid rhythm, like it had just remembered how to beat.

He inhaled sharply. The air tasted cleaner, sharper, like the first breath of the spring solstice. Every sound around him sharpened—the rustle of leaves overhead, the distant birdsong, the creak of Doran's staff against the forest floor.

He blinked again, and the haze that had clouded his mind for years vanished. His limbs no longer felt heavy, his thoughts no longer slow. The fog that had draped itself over his soul had lifted, leaving him fully awake for the first time in what felt like a lifetime.

Blood surged through his veins, filling him with a

wild, reckless sense of vitality. He felt alive again—truly, fully alive. The exhaustion that had plagued him melted away as though it had never existed. His pulse thrummed in his ears. His muscles tensed with the thrill of renewed strength, daring him to run, to leap, to fight.

The air shifted, and suddenly, he was staring into a pair of eyes he knew better than his own. Wide, shocked, and vividly green. The same eyes that had haunted his dreams for years.

"Mal?" He breathed her name like a prayer. Only this time, she answered.

Maleficent stared back at him, her expression one of disbelief. Neither of them moved. They stood frozen in the strange space between memory and reality.

Phillip was touching her. Phillip could see her. And for a terrifying, beautiful moment, Phillip thought she might be a ghost—some lingering spirit sent to torment him with what he had lost.

It didn't matter. The surreal her was just as breathtaking as the real one. If she was dead, he would follow her to the afterworld.

But then he saw the way the others stared at her too—the way their gazes flickered between her and him.

She wasn't a ghost.

She was real.

"You..." Phillip's voice faltered, his hand still cradling

hers as if afraid she would vanish again. "You're really here."

Mal shook her head slowly. She gasped in a shaky breath, as if she, too, couldn't believe what she was seeing. "You are supposed to be dead."

Phillip's hand tightened around hers, the ache in his scar fading into the background as warmth spread through his hand, up his arm, and through his chest. "I'm not. I'm here. I'm right here."

Mal let out a choked sound, her body shaking from the revelation. Then she yanked her hand away from him, turned on her heel, and stormed off.

CHAPTER SEVEN

$\mathcal{M}$al's whole body trembled, trembled with absolute fury. Her magic burned hot under her skin as she stormed deeper into the forest. Every step was fueled by rage. And all the rage was directed at Aurora.

She was going to kill the bitch. That prissy bitch of a princess. She was a pritch, that's what she was.

That pritch had come into her and Phillip's lives and tried to make a mess of their friendship. Then she'd tried to drive a wedge between their love. Why? Mal knew Aurora didn't love Phillip. At times she wondered if the pritch even liked him.

And now Mal discovered that Aurora had somehow kept them apart for years. Three years of solitude. Three years of heart sickness. Three years of living in darkness and wanting—begging—to be swallowed whole by it. Meanwhile, Phillip had been hearty and whole—and with her, the pritch.

War. It was going to be war. And Mal would delight in burning the castle and its pritch to the ground.

The forest stirred with her fury. Mal's presence made the air hum. The flora shied away from her path, bending backwards as though afraid to touch the searing heat of her rage. Her fists were clenched at her sides. Her claws bit into her palms. Her skin burned with the need for vengeance. But just as the heat ignited, she felt a cool touch on her forearm.

His touch.

It had always instantly cooled her anger, while at the same time igniting a different kind of heat within her—a slow, smoldering warmth that took root deep in her chest. Mal came to a shaky stop, her breath catching as she let the familiar sensation of him wash over her.

It had been so long since she'd been touched. So long since she'd let herself be touched. So long since she admitted that she needed affection.

And then the worst thing happened.

It started to rain.

The rain only touched the corners of her eyes. It pooled there before trailing down her cheeks. Then it fell in thin lines to her chin.

Mal never cried. She hadn't shed a tear since the day

Phillip had disappeared from her world. That day was always hazy in her mind, a blur of confusion and numbness. But the loss—that soul-deep ache—had been real. It had haunted her every day since, hollowing her out from the inside.

But now, as if the grief had never existed, that crushing weight lifted from her chest. Because Phillip—her Phillip—was standing here, alive. His hands were on her, wiping away her tears.

"How?" Her voice cracked, and she had to try again. "How is this possible?"

The warmth of his hands sent shivers through her. With the realization of what his presence meant, a new wave of emotions surged to the surface—anger, confusion, disbelief. She yanked her hands free, slapping his touch away with a sharp sting.

"How could you do this to me? Where have you been? How are you alive?"

Phillip only grinned, the corners of his mouth curling in that same maddening, boyish way that had always infuriated her—and enchanted her. "There's my fire. How I missed that temper."

"Don't you dare," Mal hissed.

He reached for her again. Every rational part of her screamed to pull away. But her body betrayed her.

She went to him. How could she not? He was right here, standing before her, solid and real. The yearning she'd buried deep in her heart surged forward like a wave crashing on the shore.

But not without consequences.

She punched him in the chest, hard enough to make her knuckles protest. Phillip didn't even grunt. His grin widened as if the hit had been expected, even welcomed.

"How could you pretend to die?" she sobbed, her voice cracking under the weight of her emotions. "How could you leave me like that?"

"I would never die without telling you first." Phillip cupped her face again, brushing his thumb over her cheek softly. So softly, as if she might shatter beneath his touch.

Doran stepped out of the shadows, his presence steady and calm as always. "Neither of you were dead. You were both under a curse. It appeared you could no longer see or hear each other. Or even hear about each other. Everyone else could see you—hear you—but when I tried to speak of Phillip to you, it was as if the words were swallowed whole. And the same happened when I spoke of you to Phillip."

The pieces of the puzzle fell into place. The strange, muffled words, the hazy memories, the inexplicable emptiness that had gnawed at her heart for years—all of it made sense now.

"It was Aurora. She did this."

"Aurora?" Phillip screwed his brows. "She's human. She doesn't have any power."

"Don't you dare defend her," Mal snapped like a blade embedding itself in a chest cavity.

"I'm not defending her. I'm telling you, she couldn't have done this. Rory doesn't have any power."

"Convenient excuse."

Phillip took a step closer, his voice low and patient, though it was edged with weariness. "The last time anyone saw a Fairy Godmother was at the sea princess Ariel's sixteenth birthday—years before our curse could've happened."

"Meanwhile, I've been in this forest, thinking you were dead, and she's been parading around with you at her side."

"I've been at war, keeping you safe."

"Whose idea was it to go to the borderlands?"

Phillip opened his mouth and then closed it. But not before looking in the direction of the castle.

"You've spent years with her, blind to everything she's been doing. How can you stand there and take her side?"

"I'm not taking her side," Phillip said, his voice rising now, matching her anger.

"You were supposed to be mine. Instead, you ended up hers."

Phillip reached out for her. Mal didn't give him the

chance to catch her. She couldn't. Her heart was too full, too raw with everything she'd held inside for the past three years. She felt like she was unraveling, and she needed to get away—needed space to breathe before the weight of her emotions consumed her entirely. She turned on her heel. And she ran.

CHAPTER EIGHT

*P*hillip cursed softly under his breath as he watched Mal disappear into the forest. Her horns gleamed in the fading light like crescent moons. A knot of frustration twisted in his chest, but beneath it burned relief, joy, and a fierce, aching gratitude.

She was alive. Mal, with her fire, her fury, her sharp edges and untamed heart, was alive.

His heart was a bouncing bean inside his chest. The vital organ was light and full for the first time in years. His blood rushed hot through his veins, his mind clear, his senses alive. It felt like spring after a long, frozen winter.

He was done standing still. Done waiting. She was

here. They were here. And nothing—not curses, not misunderstandings—would keep him from her now.

Phillip sprinted after Mal. He wove through the forest as though it were an old friend. The trees, familiar and towering, whispered their encouragement as he passed, their branches swaying with approval, recognizing him as someone who belonged here. Vines unfurled, and the underbrush parted, creating a path as the flora urged him forward.

His hands pumped at his sides. His skin burned with a desire that was equal parts longing and urgency. The leaves above him rustled on the breeze, rooting him on to close the distance.

He reached her cabin, tucked snugly between two ancient oaks. Its ivy-covered walls were as wild and stubborn as the woman who lived inside. Phillip didn't bother knocking. He never had before. Not even when her Guardian mother was alive.

Morwyn would simply smile and cock her head toward the back door. Phillip would race from the front door to the back, springing out to find his friend, his beloved, his soul mate.

He shoved the front door open and stepped inside. Immediately, he missed the old Guardian's presence. For a brief time, Morwyn had been like a mother to him. Tending to his wounds when he fell from a tree. Offering council as he began to take on his duties as

Prince Regent. Giving advice as she saw the young man falling desperately in love with her obstinate daughter.

The obstinate scent of Mal hit him first—a heady blend of oak sap, wood smoke, and wildflowers. It wrapped around him like a long-lost embrace, stirring memories of stolen moments beneath the stars, whispered promises made in the quiet dark. His chest tightened painfully at the familiarity of it.

Phillip's gaze swept the room. It was the same space he remembered, but changed. There were more plants now, growing along the walls and creeping across the floor like sentries. The hearth glowed with embers, casting soft golden light that flickered over the rough-hewn furniture. It was cozy, but there was a lingering sadness in the air, a weight that hadn't been there before when he'd visited as a child and young man.

Mal stood in the center of the room, her back straight, her jaw tight, her green eyes flashing with fury. She looked like a storm given form—wild, beautiful, dangerous. Her magic thrummed in the air around her, alive and restless, like the wood of the cabin was feeding off her emotions.

Phillip couldn't help it. He grinned. Gods, she was beautiful.

"You really didn't waste any time, did you? Running after me like a fool."

Phillip stepped closer, undeterred by the fire in her

voice. If anything, it delighted him. Mal in a fury was a sight to behold—fierce, untamed, irresistible. "Wouldn't be the first time."

She crossed her arms, glaring at him. "You're different. You used to believe in the forest. In its magic. In the idea that humans and fae could live side by side. Now your people are killing the land we both swore to protect."

Phillip's grin faded. "I didn't know. I was off fighting, trying to keep the kingdom safe. I thought everyone here was... safe."

"You left," she accused.

"Because I thought you were dead. Now I'm back. It will stop. I will stop it."

"Will you stop the wedding too?" Mal's gaze didn't soften. If anything, her green eyes burned brighter. "I saw the ring, Phillip. Your mother's engagement ring. Aurora's still wearing it."

"I didn't give her that ring. My mother did when Rory was a child. There has only ever been one woman in my heart."

Mal's breath hitched, but she held her ground, her arms still crossed tightly over her chest. "You're still going to marry her?"

Phillip shook his head, closing the distance between them. "No, Mal. I told you both three years ago. I told

Aurora I loved you. I told you both we were going to figure it all out together."

"Then the curse... And you don't find that suspicious? That the curse fell exactly when you told her you'd chosen me?"

Phillip exhaled slowly, brushing his thumb along her jaw, the familiar feel of her skin grounding him. "I don't care about suspicion. Not right now. I've spent three years without you. Three years thinking I'd never see you again. I'll be damned if I let another second go by without doing this."

It wasn't a tentative kiss. Nor a careful one. It was fierce, desperate, like a man drowning who had finally found air. His hands cradled her face, his fingers threaded into her dark hair, holding her to him as if afraid she might slip away again.

Mal resisted, her fists curling against his chest. Didn't matter to him. She could say no all she wanted, but he knew her. Knew her body. Knew what they both wanted.

As though on cue, with a soft, broken sound, Mal's body melted into his. Her arms slid around his neck, pulling him closer. Her magic flared between them, warm and wild, wrapping them both in a fire that started at the place where their chests met and ignited from their toes to their heads in one blast.

Phillip felt whole. Alive. Home.

Mal let out a shaky breath, her hands still clinging to him. "If you ever leave me again, I will kill you."

"Gods, I've missed you." Phillip smiled, pressing a soft kiss to her brow.

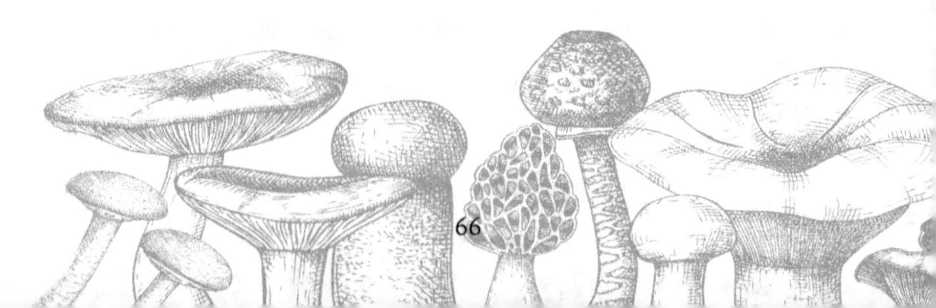

CHAPTER NINE

The world tilted beneath Mal's feet as the weight of Phillip's presence crashed into her. He was alive. He was real, standing in front of her, breathing the same air, touching her with hands she thought she'd never feel again. The deep and gnawing hollow ache that had taken root in her chest over the years began to fill, too fast and too suddenly. It overwhelmed her, made her dizzy.

Her knees wobbled. The edges of the room blurred. The ground went unsteady beneath her boots. The ceiling above spun around her. She tried to breathe, tried to steady herself, but it felt like the walls were closing in.

Too much, not enough.

It felt like her body was caught between what was real and what was impossible. More than she could handle. Yet less than she needed.

Before she crumbled into a heap, Phillip was there. Strong arms wrapped around her, pulling her close to him, steadying her against his chest. His familiar scent washed over her—smoke and leather. That was him. That was her Phillip. It really was him.

Mal braced her hands against his chest. Phillip didn't let go. If anything, he held her tighter, tucking her back into his heart where she belonged. The space fit snugly, like she'd never left. Like it had never been occupied by another.

"I've got you. You don't have to be strong right now, Mal. Not with me. Not anymore."

His words slipped under her defenses. They unraveled the walls she had built around her heart brick by brick. She sagged against him, her breath hitching as the weight of everything—her grief, her anger, her longing—came crashing down all at once.

"You can lean on me," Phillip whispered, his lips brushing her temple. "I'm strong enough to hold you."

Mal surrendered. She let her walls fall and wrapped herself around him. Her body trembled like a fortress taking a strike from a battering ram. Her face pressed into his chest. The strength that had held her together for so long ebbed away, leaving her trembling as the tears came—hot and unrelenting. They spilled from her eyes like enemies breaching the gates, overwhelming her with their relentless advance.

She cried for the years lost. For the battles she'd fought alone. For the love she had almost forfeited to time and absence. She cried for the weight she had carried, the shield she had borne, the loneliness that had hollowed her out until she felt more weapon than woman.

Here, in her Phillip's arms, she let it all go. Her burdens dropped like a sword to the ground. Her heart was no longer a battlefield but a sanctuary. Phillip held her tighter, his warmth soaking into her, filling the cracks she hadn't dared acknowledge until this moment. In his embrace, she found her truce, her peace.

His hands stroked her back in soothing circles. His touch was patient and tender. His lips followed the trail of her tears, kissing each one away with reverence, as though her tears were something sacred.

"I love you. I've always loved you. I'll never leave you again. Not by my own power or anyone else's."

Mal whimpered, her sharp tongue silenced. She softened under the fierce press of his kisses. She melted into him, her magic flickering gently around them, a reflection of her surrender.

Phillip swept her off her feet with ease. He cradled

her against his chest like she weighed nothing at all. Mal let him. She gave herself over to him fully, trusting him with a depth that no one else had ever earned. With Phillip, she didn't have to be the fierce protector, the tough-as-claws leader. She didn't have to carry the world on her shoulders.

In his arms, she was safe. She could set her burdens down. She could let go.

Her prince carried her through the cabin. The quiet crackle of the hearth and the scent of wood smoke wrapped around them like a cocoon. When he laid her on the bed, she uncurled from him, open and vulnerable for his next advance.

With Phillip, she didn't need control. She didn't need to fight. Here, she could follow, knowing he would never lead her anywhere but where she was meant to be.

"I want this off."

Mal did as she was told. She reached for the buttons on her frock. Once it was loosened, she pulled it over her head.

"I get to learn you all over again." Phillip's grin was wide. His human incisors gleamed in the pale moon's light, casting him in the glow of a wolf. He frowned, his tooth letting go of his lower lip. "Your breasts are bigger."

"They're the same size."

Phillip cocked his head to the side as though he disagreed.

"Perhaps you've fondled someone with breasts smaller than mine."

He was over her in an instant. Mal's back hit the mattress with a welcoming thud. She tilted her head back, giving her prince her neck.

"I have never in my life touched another set."

Mal opened her mouth to speak.

Phillip's glare shushed her. "Don't you dare speak her name."

Now it was Mal biting her lip.

"I am yours. And you are mine. That is the way the world made us. I would have never broken that vow to you. I will never."

The debate about breast sizes was over.

Phillip peeled the rest of her clothing from her body. Mal lay pliant under his attack on her clothing. When he had her completely naked, he parted her thighs. She didn't squirm as she had the first time he'd done this when they were still learning each other's bodies and pleasures. For weeks, this had been all they'd done—set their mouths and tongues against the other's secret places.

When Phillip's lips met her secret place, Mal was

reminded that he knew everything about her. She arched off the bed, pushing her core into his erudite tongue. He hummed his approval over her clit.

Mal threaded her hands into his hair. Phillip pressed her thighs farther open, pushing his shoulders between her to hold her down. He did not come up for air once. Instead, he dove his nose between her folds, inhaling deeply before licking and suckling the constant flow of wetness gathering at her center. She reached her pleasure embarrassingly fast.

Her heels pressed into the mattress. She tried to bring her knees together to ease the onslaught of the spasms. Phillip was having none of that.

He held her down with hands under her hips. He pressed his shoulders into her thighs to prevent them from closing. He pushed his tongue deeper into her core to give her muscles something to contract around.

Only when the contractions ebbed did he release his hold on her. Phillip lifted his head, licking his lips. Then he licked the trickle seeping from between her thighs for good measure.

"I need you," Mal said, reaching for him.

"You have me," he said, tugging off his shirt and trousers.

He prowled up her body. Mal dug her claws into his shoulders. His mouth found hers. Mal tasted her honey on his lips. His hands explored every curve and hollow of her. Mal let herself fall fully into the moment—into him.

That first orgasm had broken her into tiny pieces. But for the first time in years, she felt whole.

CHAPTER TEN

Mal shattered in Phillip's arms. This time it was around his length. Phillip gritted his teeth and held his release at bay. He was not done. He would never be done with her.

They'd had to take it slowly when he'd pressed just the tip inside her. Three years apart and her channel had become snug. It was like the first time all over again. Only better. Because this time Phillip knew exactly how to get his love wet.

When they were young, he was all too eager to get inside of the wondrous creature that was Maleficent. There had been a few winces and sharp intakes of breath as he fumbled his way into her channel. This time, Phillip took pleasure in working himself in slowly, inch by inch, while she begged him for more, harder, faster. Once she caught her breath from the second orgasm, he would give her that—and more.

Phillip held Mal close, his arms wrapped tightly around her as if, by sheer will alone, he could keep her there forever. That first kiss of the reunion had shattered the lethargy that had weighed on him for three long years. The fog that had dulled his senses, the exhaustion that had seeped into his bones—gone, as if it had never existed. He felt awake, truly awake, for the first time in what felt like a lifetime.

It was more than their kiss. More than the orgasms. It was magic. The kind read about in fairy tales. The kind no one believed in until it happened right before their eyes.

The world tasted sweeter with Mal's lips against his. The air smelled fresher with each breath they shared. He could feel it—his blood rushing hot and fast through his veins, his heart thundering in his chest. That first kiss had made his soul sing, reigniting every part of him that had withered without her.

He smiled against her lips now. The joy was so fierce it made his chest ache. This was what it meant to live.

Mal's hard body was soft and yielding under him. He'd always marveled that she was the daughter of a tree. Her skin was the rich color of the earth. Her attitude was tough as bark. But Phillip had always seen the softness of her. He'd always seen past the fire and steel she wielded against the rest of the world to protect her folk as their Guardian. It was only in his arms that she didn't have to be fierce.

When Mal was with Phillip, she set her burdens down and played as a child, laughed as a young girl, loved as a grown woman. With him, she didn't have to carry the weight of the forest or protect everyone around her. Here, with him, she could rest. She could give in. And Phillip knew that was the rarest gift he could give her: trust, the ability for this great Guardian to surrender. Even if just for a time.

He kissed her deeper, pressing his erection as far as he could reach into her core. She gasped, her inner muscles tightening around him again. Not in orgasm, just in delight.

He tasted the salt of her tears, giving gratitude to each one she blessed him with. Her scent—earthy, wild, and tinged with something floral—wrapped around him like a spell, grounding him as he ground his hips into her. He inhaled deeply, savoring the scent of their lovemaking, committing it to memory.

Phillip hadn't been born hungry for power or war. He had grown up knowing that duty came first—that his role was to serve his people and keep peace. The only conquest he had ever desired, the only victory that had ever mattered to him, was winning Mal.

From the time they were young, he had studied her with the precision of a tactician, searching for the cracks in her formidable armor. He'd found those cracks hidden beneath her strength and sharp edges. For all her power, Mal craved care. She longed for someone strong enough to stand beside her. Someone she didn't have to carry. Someone who would carry her when she grew weary.

Phillip knew this truth well. He had learned it wasn't just Mal who craved this care; many powerful women like her did. Show them a steady, capable hand, and they would bend willingly—not to submission, but to trust.

Phillip didn't want to bend Mal in surrender. No, the only way he ever wanted to bend her was beneath him, atop him, on her knees facing him or with her face buried in the pillows as he buried himself inside her.

She bent her knees, pulling them up toward her armpits now. Her body was as pliant as a blade of spring grass as she welcomed him even deeper into her body. Her lips were soft beneath his. Her body was warm and pliable in his arms. Right now, she was a living contradiction to the untouchable force she showed the world. She was fire and wildness, yes, but here, in his embrace, she was also soft rain and quiet nights. She was everything, and Phillip was a man reborn.

When he'd thought she was dead, something inside him had died, too. Every day since had felt like a slow suffocation, the world dull and lifeless without her. But now... now he was in heaven as he brought her toward her third orgasm.

He knew that with each of her climaxes, her muscles would clench harder, longer. This time, she screamed while Phillip nearly choked on his tongue. Her private muscles squeezed him so hard it stole his breath.

He could hold back his pleasure no longer. Phillip tilted his head and roared his release. Once he was spent inside of her, he found her mouth. He savored the way Mal responded to him without hesitation. She clutched at his shoulders, locking her ankles over his ass as she continued to tremble and undulate against him. Her magic hummed faintly between them, brushing against his skin like a whisper, as if even her power acknowledged the connection between them.

He wasn't just holding her in his arms—he was holding her heart, her trust, her soul. It was fitting, since he'd given all those things to her the first time they'd met. Now it felt like he was being reacquainted with a part of himself he'd left behind. He swore to himself and to her that they would never be parted again.

CHAPTER ELEVEN

The warmth of the bed crashed against Mal's back as she came awake. The soft weight of blankets held her down as she gave a tentative kick in an effort to be free of them. The blankets held fast. She decided to give in. What would five more minutes of resting hurt? It wasn't as if she had anywhere to be. Anyone waiting for her.

Her parents had passed on to the Afterworld. Phillip was gone. And… wait. No. That wasn't right.

Mal ran her big toe up her calf. She felt an ache between her thighs. Not a painful ache. It was the ache she always felt after she'd lain with…

Her eyes slammed open. She reached out beside her. And came up with air. She stared at the empty place in the bed.

Panic twisted in her chest. Had it all been a dream? Had she imagined Phillip's return, his touch, the way his kiss had brought her back to life?

All around her, it was quiet—too quiet, too still. Her heart plummeted in her chest, sinking under the weight of the loneliness she thought she'd banished.

She sat up, clutching the blankets around her, her breath shaky.

Then the faintest sound. Weight upon wood. Like a footstep not wishing to disturb. The door creaked open. And there he was.

Phillip stood in the doorway. In his hands, he held a steaming mug. He gave her that soft, lopsided grin that made her heart stutter its beats. "Ah, I woke you."

He crossed the room, sat on the edge of the bed, and handed her the mug. The scent of it wafted up—rich, earthy, with a hint of sweetness. It was exactly how she liked it. Because he'd remembered every detail of what pleased her. The bruises on her skin and love bites between her thighs were testament to that.

Phillip leaned in and kissed her. Mal gave in to him without a second thought. The press of his lips was warm and lingering. Her eyes fluttered closed, savoring the kiss for a moment longer, as if storing it away for later.

She'd taken moments like these for granted. She'd forgotten the small touches, the quiet moments, the glances they shared that spoke a language only the two of them knew. She knew this man so well, and he knew her. How had she survived these last three years without her other half at her side?

She set the steaming mug on the bedside table. She threaded her warm fingers through Phillip's hair and pulled him down for the morning treat she truly wanted. He came to her. But he didn't lick into her mouth like he had all the time in the world to savor her.

Mal pulled back. Phillip winced as he looked at her. The warmth of the kiss faded into suspicion.

"You're leaving."

Phillip sighed, running a hand through his dark hair. "I owe Aurora an explanation, Mal. I can't just... disappear on her. I'm not going to break things off through a carrier pigeon note."

"So you are going back to her?"

"It's not like that. I just need to—"

"Are you still under her curse?"

"We don't know that she—"

"You must still be in her thrall if you take her word over mine."

"Mal—"

Phillip reached for her hands. Mal snatched them away. She slid out of the bed, from the side opposite Phillip. She snatched up one of the linens to cover her naked body as the heat of desire left her bones cold.

"After everything, after three years apart, you still think that pritch is innocent?"

"Pritch?"

Mal gritted her teeth instead of explaining.

"I'm not saying I don't believe you. I just—"

"Taking her side over mine."

"There are no sides, Mal. Not if you're in the vicinity. My place is next to you. Everyone else... they're just outsiders."

Mal's heart wavered. The anger in her chest flickered like a candle in the face of a door swinging open. His words settled over her like a balm, soothing the sting of her doubts. She searched his gaze, looking for any trace of dishonesty, but found none.

"Then I'm coming with you."

"That is not a good idea."

"Why not?"

"The two of you in a room..." Phillip opened his mouth. Closed it. Then just shook his head.

"I won't hurt her."

"I don't believe you."

"Yet you believe she didn't hurt me."

"Mal, let me handle this."

Mal turned away from him again. As one of the most fearsome creatures in the forests, she knew better than to give an adversary her back. But ever since she was a young sapling, she'd felt the urge to lay down her weapons before this boy so that they could share them like toys. As she grew into a girl who would become the fierce Guardian of the forest, she developed a habit of showing this young man her shoulder blades so that he could kiss them.

She felt Phillip's breath against her ear, his nose against one of her horns. Then his tongue. Involuntarily, she shuddered. Voluntarily, she pressed her back into his chest and exposed her entire collarbone.

"You remember what happens when you give me the silent treatment?"

He wrapped a hand around one horn and tugged her head back. Mal's lids grew too heavy. She couldn't keep them open under the onslaught of pleasure.

"I make you scream my name."

She pushed her chin higher into the air. Her shoulder blades pressed into him. Her chest rose into the air. Her heart was trying to do a backflip to get to the one who owned it.

She was airborne. She crashed into the mattress. Her back hit the pillows. Her thighs were tossed over Phillip's shoulders. His tongue made good on his threat. It wasn't long before he had her screaming.

The battle was lost before she'd picked up any arms. She couldn't have. Not when he pinned her arms beneath her. Long after she gave in, he didn't stop. Not until she whimpered and begged. But her words formed no concrete meanings. She wasn't sure they were actual words. Only pleas.

Rising up, Phillip licked his lips. Mal got a thrill knowing that her essence was all over him. She wanted him to go and see Aurora now. She wanted that pritch to see the evidence of Mal's claim on him.

Phillip smiled, brushing a thumb over the exposed flesh between her thighs. Her core wept at his touch. "It will always be you and me. That's simply how the world made us."

Mal huffed but leaned forward, pressing one last kiss to his lips—slow, deliberate, a warning wrapped in affection. When she pulled back, she rested her forehead against his. "Be careful," she commanded. "Come back to me."

"I promise I'll be back before evening. You'll see—everything will be fine."

CHAPTER TWELVE

The ride back to the castle was an easy affair. Phillip's steed was clearly happy with his stay in the Enchanted Forest. The grass there was greener, the air fresher, and the magic did something to pick up both man's and horse's steps. Though Phillip was certain it was a certain magical woman who had lightened his step.

Now he pushed open the heavy doors to the council chamber. Conversations halted as his shadow caught the morning light. The council members turned to glance at him. Their faces were a mixture of surprise and discomfort—he wasn't expected. That much was clear.

He scanned the room and caught the soldier's voice mid-report. Phillip recognized him immediately. It was one of the men who had tried bulldozing the sacred tree ring. The man stood stiffly, speaking with the clipped tones of someone carefully treading the line between truth and what the council wanted to hear.

"Progress was... halted. A fairy appeared at the site. She... she obstructed our efforts to clear the area."

There was no distortion as the words traveled unobstructed to Phillip's ears. No muffled syllables. The soldier's voice came through clear, unclouded by the cursed effects that had obscured Maleficent's name in the past.

"Powerful?" Lord Queros asked. "And yet you returned unscathed?"

The soldier hesitated. "Yes, Your Grace. She... she stopped the machines but did not harm us directly."

"These creatures are more beasts of the field than anything. I'm sure the fact you escaped was an oversight. We need to push forward. End this blight infesting the edge of our borders, borders that should not exist."

Phillip's hand rested against the pommel of his sword, not out of necessity but to steady himself. Before he could interject, Aurora's voice cut through the air, sharper than he'd ever heard it.

"Prince Phillip has secured the borders where we were in danger. The Forest Folk are making no advance. Our men weren't harmed. This does not change the plan that our prince, soon to be our king, has set out for us. Has it?"

The council members exchanged glances, some straightening in their seats, as if startled by her sudden change in tone. Phillip felt the shift, too—a subtle tension that set his teeth on edge. Aurora never raised her voice. Not to him, not to anyone. She was always sweet, always composed. Her words had come out too quick, too hard. Lord Queros pursed his lips together so firmly that Phillip suspected a lemon might pop out of him.

Aurora's gaze snapped to Phillip. He saw the change as if a mask had slipped back into place. Her expression softened instantly, her lips curving into the delicate, practiced smile. It was the first time since knowing her that his interest was piqued. But that pique never left the ground.

"There you are, my love. I have to assume we have you to thank for the diplomacy in this matter?" Aurora rose gracefully from her chair, smoothing the folds of her gown. She moved toward him, her every step measured, her gaze warm—too warm. "I assume that's where you've been all night, working hard on your diplomatic mission."

Phillip kept his expression carefully neutral. He was looking for it now—the subtle shift, the crack in her serene exterior. "I was in the forests all night meeting with old friends."

Aurora's smile faltered, almost imperceptibly. Just a flicker, but enough to send a prickle of unease down his spine. He'd seen that flicker before. Felt that prickle whenever he brought up Mal. Aurora's jealousy was on full display to his eyes only.

Why would she prickle if she thought Mal was dead?

"Oh?" she said lightly. "Which friends?"

"You remember Doran?"

The corners of her mouth softened, almost like a valve being released. The jealousy-prickle flickered out.

"The one that's a tree?"

"He's a dryad."

"Oh, right. Forgive my ignorance of your forest creatures. My kingdom was surrounded by the sea and its kind. The sea folk rarely came out of the water."

"Having a dryad like Doran sitting on the council would eliminate any misunderstandings like the one yesterday."

Lord Queros slammed his hands down on the armrests of his chair as though he were about to rise. A glance around the table showed he had no support. No one else was half or even a quarter out of their seat.

"You are the sovereign," she said with a graceful incline of her head, the words smooth but hollow. They sat wrong in Phillip's ears, as if she were reciting a line she didn't believe.

Before he could press her further, Aurora's voice sounded again, gentle, like a lullaby.

"You look tired, Phillip. Are you sure you shouldn't rest from your… excursion?"

The words carried a strange weight, an almost imperceptible tug. His head throbbed faintly. The kind of dull head ache that made him want to take to his bed for a nap. There it was again—that familiar pressure in his fingertip, that subtle ache that hadn't left him since the day Mal was taken from him.

Phillip inhaled slowly. The scent of Mal was still on his tongue. It gave him a spark of energy. But he didn't let that show. Instead, he allowed Aurora to take his arm and lead him out of the council room. This visit, he realized, was going to take longer than he'd planned.

CHAPTER THIRTEEN

The forest hummed with life in the late afternoon sun. Its vibrant energy washed over Mal as she stepped out of her cabin. She'd taken her time getting out of bed after Phillip's departure. Mostly out of necessity. Her prince had ridden her rough and hard last night… and this morning. Mal had needed a little more than average recovery time for her sensitive parts.

A light breeze carried the mingling scents of wildflowers and damp moss. The forest itself breathed a carefree sigh at her appearance. The towering trees swayed lazily, their leaves rustling like children raising their voices now that it was playtime. Even the smallest creatures seemed to sense they could let loose. Birds trilled wildly from the canopy above, their songs untamed and jubilant, while a pair of fox kits darted out of their den, tumbling and wrestling with no care for decorum.

The alert tension that had clung to the forest during her absence dissolved as she walked farther into the clearing. The vines, once coiled like sentries around the perimeter, now relaxed their hold on the earth, stretching languidly toward the sun. Flowers tilted their faces upward, as though they had been waiting for her warmth to coax them into full bloom. The forest exhaled now that the Guardian had returned.

Mal felt the weight of her role settle over her shoulders. But today, it wasn't crushing. She could bear it. Phillip's return to her life made the burden less daunting. His love was a quiet strength that flowed into her like a river replenishing the land.

Last night, in the sanctuary of his arms, she had allowed herself to unravel, to lay down her armor and simply be. Only with Phillip could she allow herself to be who she truly was at her core: a woman with vulnerabilities, fears, and longings.

She had gorged herself on the strength of her prince. All night long, his hands had traced her back, steadying her when she felt like she might fall apart. She had drawn from his well of patience, his quiet resolve. And now, with the forest stirring around her, she felt renewed. She could carry an extra load today, knowing that tonight, he would return to her and let his strength fill her once more.

Her boots crunched over twigs and leaves as she approached the heart of the forest. Vines curled and unfurled, recognizing her magic. They brushed against her skin like old friends greeting her after too long apart.

She felt it again—power thrumming in her veins. The sluggishness that had weighed her down these past three years was gone, replaced by sharp, focused energy. But the warmth that usually accompanied being home was tainted by unease. As much as the forest welcomed her back, the council she was about to face would be far less forgiving.

When Mal entered the clearing, the forest council was already gathered—sprites with gossamer wings glittering in the sun, dryads with skin like bark, and fae elders whose faces seemed older than the trees they guarded. Their murmurs quieted the moment she stepped into view. The tension in the air thickened.

"You've returned," said one of the dryads, his eyes dark and suspicious. His voice rustled like autumn leaves. "How convenient."

The words weren't an accusation outright, but they were close enough. Others nodded, their expressions unreadable but clearly guarded. Only the ironwoods and redwoods, the towering sentinel trees of the forest, stood steadfast. Their presence, resolute and unyielding, signaled silent allegiance as they came to stand directly behind Mal. It was a reminder that she had the strength of the enchanted woods at her back.

"I was cursed. What part of that do you not understand?"

"You've been... absent for years, Maleficent."

"Three years, to be exact. Now the curse is broken. And now that it is, we need to act. Aurora won't stop until the forest is ashes beneath her feet."

The council exchanged glances—some thoughtful, others doubtful. The dryads, rooted in their long memories and unshakable wisdom, seemed to lean toward agreement. The sprites, however, fluttered anxiously, their delicate wings catching slivers of light as they hovered close together. They weren't built for war. They were creatures of joy and mischief. Their unease was evident in the way they glanced at one another, uncertain and hesitant.

The fae, ever elegant and enigmatic, were visibly divided. Some stood with arms crossed, their expressions set in icy determination, their gazes promising allegiance to Mal's cause. Others, though, shifted on their feet, eyes averted, clearly torn between loyalty to the forest and fear of what conflict might bring.

"We must consider all options," Doran offered. "There may still be a path toward peace. A parlay."

"Parlay?" Mal echoed, her voice sharp with disbelief. "You want to talk? You think Aurora's going to sit down and sip tea with me after cursing me with some kind of sleep-walking spell?"

A young sprite leaned forward, his lavender face still carrying some of the baby fat of his youth. "Perhaps it was just a misunderstanding and—"

"She made me think my true love was dead." Mal's voice cut through him like a blade. "She's poison wrapped in silk. How can you not see that? How can you think, after everything she's done, that she's capable of reason? Has she cursed you all too? Because that's the only explanation I can think of for why you'd be this blind."

Silence followed her words, heavy and uncomfortable. The council members glanced at one another as if searching for someone brave enough to challenge her. A flutter of wings broke the tense silence. Mal turned, her sharp gaze tracking the sound.

A pigeon swooped into the clearing, its feathers catching the dappled sunlight as it spiraled down toward them. The bird landed gracefully in front of one of the sprites, who bent to retrieve a small scroll tied to the bird's leg.

"Message from the castle," the sprite said, unfastening the roll of parchment.

Mal stared at the bird. Then at the scroll. The sprite cocked its head to the side and then looked up at Mal.

"It's for you."

A message from the castle? A carrier pigeon sent with a message from the castle for her? She was going to kill him.

CHAPTER FOURTEEN

The soft knock at the door pulled Phillip from his thoughts. He straightened, his pulse steady but his mind alert. He bade the person on the other side of the door enter and then failed to hide his jolt of surprise at his guest.

Aurora stepped into the room, a picture of grace and poise. She smiled, a delicate curve of her lips that had always made him feel protective of her. Right now, all he could do was stare at her hands—her knuckles, to be precise. In all the years she'd lived in this castle, she had never once knocked on any door before coming in.

"You don't look tired." Her words were aimed more to herself. Her chin even dipped a bit as she regarded him. A small frown marred her brow. Then it smoothed itself out as she smiled brighter.

Phillip took an involuntary step back. "It's been an eventful day. I was just about to turn in."

Aurora stepped closer, placing her hands lightly on his chest. Phillip fought the instinct to pull away, forcing his muscles to stay relaxed. The touch was gentle, but it carried weight—a weight that felt heavy, tiresome.

Aurora tilted her head, looking up at him with wide, innocent eyes that he now knew better than to trust. "I wanted to thank you, Phillip."

"Thank me?"

"For welcoming me into your world. Into your castle after my father's unfortunate demise. For allowing me to sit beside you on your throne even before we've said our vows to one another."

Her gaze flicked toward the bed—just a glance, but enough to set Phillip's pulse on edge. She had never hinted at more between them than their public partnership. Tonight, the unspoken invitation hung in the air.

"I know someone else still lingers in your heart. But we'll be married soon. Perhaps it's time to bury her memory."

Phillip's smile remained firmly in place—a smile honed through years of diplomacy. He took her hands, moving them off his chest. "Rory, you've always been a trusted partner and a valuable friend."

"Soon I'll be your wife."

As ever, Phillip neither agreed nor disagreed with the statement. "Soon is not tonight."

He kept his hands around hers just long enough to make the gesture feel like an acknowledgment rather than a rejection. Then he released her and took a deliberate step back.

"You're right—it's been a long day. Rest is what we both need."

"Goodnight, Rory," he said, moving to the door and holding it open for her. "I'll see you in the morning."

Before he could close the door on this discussion, she turned back to him. Those rosy pink lips parted. Her gaze dipped to his mouth. Her head leaned in slightly, as though she had the thought to kiss him.

Phillip's lips parted to warn her off. There was no need. Aurora straightened and pressed her lips together in a smile. She bobbed a curtsy—another action he had never once seen her do to another living soul—and started down the hall.

Phillip closed the door behind her with a quiet click, locking it with a smooth press of his thumb. He exhaled, tension bleeding from his shoulders as he leaned against the door. The scent of lavender still clung faintly to the air.

He knew then, with cold certainty, that Aurora's mask was slipping. Whatever game she was playing, it was going to reach its conclusion soon. But first he had another dangerous maze to traverse.

Phillip barely had time to catch his breath after shutting the door when something sharp whizzed past his ear. He ducked just in time to avoid a thorn as thick as his thumb hurtling through the air. It missed his ear by a hair and embedded itself in the wood behind him with a muted thunk.

A puff of shimmering pollen clouded the air, floating toward him in a golden haze. He twisted to the side, batting the air away just as thick vines slithered through the open window, reaching for him like eager serpents. With a low curse, he lunged forward, grabbing the writhing form just outside the window.

His hands closed around Mal's shoulders, pulling her inside. She struggled against him, her magic alive and buzzing under her skin like a wild current.

"Hush," Phillip whispered, struggling to keep his grip on her as she kicked and twisted. "Hush or she'll hear you."

"Oh, I'll make sure she hears us," Mal hissed. "I'm going to make you scream."

Phillip's grin was wide and unapologetic. His lips twisted when Mal grabbed his cock. The heat of her palm was welcome. The malice curling her fingers was not.

"That putrid princess is going to hear you scream my name."

Mal's snarl was feral. It only delighted Phillip further. He'd missed her fire—her untamed, wild spirit. Seeing her now in full fury made his heart swell. He had forgotten how exhilarating it was to be on the receiving end of Maleficent's wrath.

She sank to her knees. He let her. He didn't tell her that Aurora had taken over his mother's bedroom down the hall. The queen had had her bedroom sound proofed with a spell so as not to hear the lovers her husband brought into his bed most nights. Aurora wouldn't hear a thing.

She wouldn't hear Mal unbuttoning his trousers. She wouldn't hear his intake of breath as the woman who owned his heart released his cock from its cage of linens. She wouldn't hear his moans of *Yes* and *More* and *Gods, please, Mal,* as the love of his life staked her claim on him with her tongue. And when he reached his peak and roared his release, Aurora was the last thing on his mind as Mal swallowed him whole—body, seed, and soul.

Blessedly, Mal gave him a moment to collect himself, and his breath, and rebuttoned his trousers before she lambasted into him again.

"A pigeon?"

Phillip chuckled, hauling her into his arms despite

her writhing. "I didn't want to break my word to you. I promised I'd be back tonight, and I wasn't going to make it without sending word."

"You also promised to break up with her. From the looks of things—like her trying to invite herself into your bed—you didn't follow through."

Phillip kissed Mal before she could say another word. His lips captured hers in a hungry kiss. She tasted like earth and wild magic and him. He'd missed this—missed the spark of her, missed that glowing light of passion between them, missed the way she met him with equal force, never giving an inch.

Mal bit down on his tongue, hard enough to draw a sharp hiss from him. It didn't deter him in the slightest. If anything, it only made him hungrier for her. He deepened the kiss, savoring every stolen second. When he finally pulled back, his chest heaved with breathless exhilaration.

"I think you were right. Aurora might've been the one who poisoned us."

Mal rolled her eyes, unimpressed by his delayed revelation. "Of course I'm right. You're just catching up."

Phillip brushed a stray hair from her face, curling the wayward tendril around her horn. Mal shuddered at the contact. He wished he had time to lay her down on his bed and lick her from horns to toes. But they were on a ticking time clock now that Aurora was clearly suspicious. What else could she be with that failed seduction when Phillip knew—had always known—the princess had no desire for him?

"What's the last thing you remember? The last day you saw me—what do you remember?"

Mal's brow furrowed in thought, her expression shifting as she searched her memories. She looked vulnerable, as if the past and the curse still held power over her. Then, like a spark catching flame, her eyes widened.

"A spindle," she said, the word falling from her lips like a malediction.

At the same time, Phillip breathed the same word. "A spindle."

CHAPTER FIFTEEN

The castle was eerily silent, save for the soft echo of their footsteps against the cold stone floor. Shadows stretched long in the dim torchlight, flickering as Mal followed behind Phillip through the winding halls. In the forests, Phillip always followed her. She was on his turf now.

The air was damp with the scent of old stone and the faint musk of smoldering candles. Every creak of the floorboards, every distant rustle made the hair on the back of her neck stand on end. Phillip's castle had always felt foreign to her, a place where she never truly belonged. And now she was sneaking through it with the man who would be king.

They ducked into the shadow of a pillar, pressing against jagged stone as a guard's footsteps echoed closer. Phillip's body was tense beside her, his sharp eyes fixed on the passing figure. They waited, barely breathing, until the guard's steps grew fainter and fainter and then he was out of sight.

"Do you ever get tired of keeping me a secret?"

Phillip blinked, clearly caught off guard by the question. His brow furrowed in confusion.

"I mean, here we are, sneaking around your castle. Again. It feels like I've always been this—this secret. Hidden away in the shadows while you played proper princeling with the pretty princess."

Another set of footsteps sounded from the opposite end of the hall. Phillip's eyes flicked toward the approaching guard, then back to her. He motioned for her to be silent, to wait. Mal had had enough of waiting.

With a flick of her wrist, Mal sent her magic coursing through the air like invisible tendrils. The guard's breath hitched as a shimmering haze of pollen and spores encircled his head, glimmering faintly in the light. His eyes reddened and began to water. His face contorted with sudden sneezes and gasps. The allergic reaction overwhelmed him in seconds. He stumbled backward, clutching his throat as his strength gave out, and then crumpled to the ground, incapacitated, his ragged breaths coming in shallow gasps. Then silence as he slipped into sleep.

Mal lowered her hand and turned back to Phillip. "You were saying?"

Looking down at the guard, Phillip pressed his lips together. His brows rose as though to say *What else would I have expected?* "As soon as we figure out what happened to us, as soon as we know why we were kept apart, I'll make sure everyone who didn't witness me following behind you like a puppy as a child, who was unaware of my infatuation with you as a young boy, everyone who didn't recognize my complete obsession with you as a grown man, knows that I have some warm feelings toward you. I'll shout it from the battlements. I'll have it written in the stars if it'll make you happy."

Phillip's words poured over her like sunlight breaking through the tallest tree canopy. His voice was steady and deep, carrying the weight of a love that refused to bend or falter.

Mal held herself tall, her hands clasped behind her back, her face a mask of calm indifference. She willed her body to stay still, her sharp black horns crowning her head like a queen's defiant tiara. Inside, her heart betrayed her. It hammered against her ribcage with a ferocity that mocked her composure, each beat louder than the last.

"You are the only woman I have ever loved, the only

woman I'll ever sit next to on that throne. But something—"

"Some*one*."

" — kept us apart for three years. I need to understand how and why. I won't let you be put in danger again."

There was a rawness in his voice that made her chest tighten as her heart slammed against her ribcage. Mal swallowed, her anger dissipating like fog under the sun. "Fine."

"Fine?"

She nodded.

"So can we proceed to solve this mystery now?"

"Yes."

"Excellent."

Phillip reached for her hand. Mal took his offering, denying to herself that it felt like surrender. Phillip's fingers wrapped around hers as they climbed the tower's long and winding stairs. Mal's fingers curled tightly around his, holding on as though letting go would shatter her completely.

"What finally made you believe Aurora was lying?"

"She came to my bedroom."

"That's the first time?" Mal tried to keep the accusation out of her tone. She believed Phillip when he told her he was devoted to her.

"No, she's come by a lot in the past, but she rarely knocks."

Mal managed to keep a relaxed grip on Phillip's hand. Stone crumbled beneath the fingertips where the other hand touched the wall.

"It's the first time she's ever tried to get in my bed, though."

Neither Mal nor her magic had time to react to that statement. They'd reached the door to the tower. The pulse of dark magic oozing from the cracks around the door frame made Mal recoil. The door creaked open without either of them touching it, inviting them— daring them—to come inside.

The air inside the tower was thick with enchantments, making Mal's skin prickle as she stepped through the arched doorway. Dust motes drifted lazily in the filtered light that streamed through a single narrow window. The room felt alive—bristling with the latent power of objects left to languish here.

A cracked mirror sat leaning against the wall. Its surface shimmered unnaturally, as though it were aware of their presence. The reflection within seemed to ripple, distorted by something unseen, as though it waited for someone brave—or foolish—enough to look into its glass.

On a small wooden table, a bright red cape was folded neatly, though claw marks showed that the fabric was shredded on one side. An apple, as red and glossy as freshly spilled blood, rested on a shelf, the air around it humming with dark energy. A single bite had been taken out of it. But around the white flesh, there were no brown marks of decay.

A pair of glass slippers, so delicate they looked like they would shatter with a touch, gleamed eerily from a corner. The root of each shoe bore streaks of blood at the tips where a woman's toes would have been forced to fit.

On a dresser by the far wall, a conch shell sat, its surface iridescent. The shell pulsed faintly, like it was alive. Mal's eyes lingered on it for a moment, her magic brushing against its aura. It carried whispers of the sea that filled her ears with faint echoes. There was a power within it slumbering, waiting to be awakened.

Phillip had pointed out the tower when they were children. They hadn't dared venture up the steps, not with all the dark magic inside. Phillip's father had been trying to rid the land of curses after the Fairy Godmothers had abandoned Evermore.

A cursed spindle gleamed malevolently on a pedestal. Its sharp tip caught the light like a tooth waiting to bite. In the quiet, Mal swore she heard it whisper to her. In her mind's eye, a vision flashed of that needle coming toward her.

But that was impossible. She'd never once set foot in this room.

Beside her, Phillip stepped forward, his gaze locked on the spindle. His hand lifted toward it, as though something unseen called to him, drawing him closer.

"Phillip, wait." Mal grabbed his wrist, her magic crackling between them. The pulse of her power hummed in the air, wrapping around them like a protective veil.

Phillip blinked, the trance breaking. "It feels like... it's calling me."

More and more, this scene felt like a memory. Except they hadn't been in this room. They'd been... in Aurora's rooms.

Aurora had invited them both. She wanted to show them her wedding dress. It was soon after the mantle of Guardianship had passed to Mal. Soon after, Phillip had lost his father and would take the crown. He had been expected to marry soon. Expected to marry her —Aurora.

Mal had been seething. Phillip had been calm. He'd said they would explain to Aurora how things were, that he loved Mal and couldn't marry Aurora.

The next thing Mal remembered was waking up.

"She did this," Phillip said. "She did this to us."

Mal wanted to praise the roots that he finally got it.

That they were finally on the same page. But they were no longer alone in the tower.

"Looks like the two of you are awake."

Aurora stood in the doorway framed by the sunlight, her golden hair glinting like a crown, her expression sharp and dangerous. Beside her stood an equally stunning redhead in a dress of soft sea-green. In her hands, she held a conch shell like the one on the dresser. Its surface gleamed as though freshly plucked from the ocean's depths.

"Can you believe that all that nonsense about True Love's kiss was real, Ari?"

The redhead shook her head, her long hair moving over her shoulders like octopus tendrils.

"This time, I'll make sure you stay asleep. Permanently."

Aurora turned to Ari, who lifted the shell to her red-glossed mouth and blew. Water erupted from the conch in a massive surge, rushing forward with an unstoppable force. The tower trembled under the weight of the blast.

Phillip lunged, shoving Mal aside with the force of his body. It was of no use. The waters came for them both.

The wall of water slammed into them, icy and unrelenting. It tore through the space, sweeping her and Phillip off their feet.

The water enveloped her, cold and brutal, stealing the breath from her lungs. She reached for Phillip, but the force was too great. The tower walls blurred into chaos as the wave blasted them out of the window.

They fell together, the roaring water cascading around them like a shroud. Mal's heart was a panicked drumbeat in her chest as they plummeted. Her hand brushed against Phillip's. Their fingers locked.

Mal sent out her magic. It surged, desperate to protect them. But the fall was relentless.

The world spun as they hurtled toward the forest below. The last glimpse of the tower window faded into the distance. Aurora's mocking laughter and Ariel's sinister smile lingered in Mal's mind.

And then Phillip's arms were around her. Her forever fortress against anything that dared cause her harm. The safe space she could let down her defenses and rest in. Except now, there was nothing below them except the ground coming fast as they fell from the tower.

CHAPTER SIXTEEN

*P*hillip thought heat was supposed to rise. The air was cold as they fell. It whipped at his face, tearing at his clothes as he clutched Mal tightly against him. Gravity pulled them downward with merciless speed. The ground rushed up to meet them. His only thought was simple: If this was the end, he would go down protecting her.

But Mal—his fierce, indomitable Mal—was already calling upon her forest.

Branches reached out as they plummeted. Thick boughs stretched to slow their descent. The leaves rustled like a whispered prayer, cushioning their fall.

But they were falling too fast. The branches bowed beneath their weight. One by one, the boughs snapped, sending them tumbling farther.

Below them, vines slithered through the air, wrapping tightly around their bodies, pulling taut to slow their speed. They, too, stretched thin. Trembling with effort, the vines snapped.

Mal and Phillip weren't over the earth. The dark gleam of water spread below them like a waiting abyss. Phillip's stomach dropped as they crashed into the icy depths.

The water was colder than the air. It slapped him hard, a hammer, knocking the air from his lungs, the sense from his brain. Thank the godmothers it was not enough to break his hold on his beloved.

He'd made Mal a promise. He would not break it. He would never let her go again. His promise held firm, as did his arms around her.

The water swallowed them whole, dark and frigid. For a heartbeat, Phillip struggled. The primal urge to breathe burned in his chest. Then something strange and wondrous happened.

Flora—soft, delicate plants with bioluminescent tendrils—rose from the depths to cradle them. The plants wound gently around their limbs, their glowing fronds swaying like dancers in the current, easing them into the water's embrace.

Blue vines slid over Phillip's face, covering his mouth and nose like a soft veil. Panic surged, and he thrashed, fighting against the alien sensation. His muscles burned. Water sloshed in his ears, making everything sound distant and warped.

Mal's hand found his. Her touch was steady, reassuring, even beneath the water's pressure. He turned to her, and what little breath that remained left him. And then his lungs took in more.

The same plants covered her mouth, their tendrils pulsing gently. She wasn't panicking. Her eyes, dark and steady, met his, filled with quiet trust. She pressed her palm against his chest, her magic thrumming in soft waves through her touch, urging him to calm.

Phillip hesitated, then forced himself to inhale slowly. The plant's fronds shifted, releasing a cool, refreshing breath into his lungs. It was pure, concentrated oxygen. The plants had drawn in the carbon dioxide. He exhaled and transformed it into what he needed to breathe. The burn in his chest eased, the tension in his muscles unwound.

The plants shifted in tandem, wrapping gently around Phillip and Mal to pull them through the current. As they drifted underwater and away from the castle, the water grew warmer, the current softer, guiding them into the sanctuary of the Enchanted Forest.

Phillip's gaze never left Mal. He drew her close. She came willingly, sliding into his arms like she belonged there. Because she did.

Words weren't necessary—not that they could speak through the strange plants feeding them breath. Mal's fingers curled into the fabric of his tunic, her hold firm and reassuring. Both of them knew without saying that no force—no curse, no magic—would ever separate them again.

Aurora had tried to kill them both. Not just him—but Mal. The woman who held his heart, who had fought her way back to him after three long years of separation.

Aurora had tried to kill her. There was no explaining that away, no justification. The truth seared through him like a blade: Aurora wasn't the victim in this story. She was the villain. Phillip had played the fool, blind to the danger she posed.

They surfaced with gasps. Water streamed down his face and burned in his lungs. Mal slipped from his arms and climbed out of the water with graceful ease. Droplets gleamed on her skin like moonlit jewels. Phillip followed, feeling the weight of his drenched clothes dragging against him, but nothing could slow the tempest brewing inside his chest.

As they reached the edge of the water, forest folk emerged from the shadows; sprites, dryads, and other creatures of the Enchanted Forest. It was clear they'd heard what had happened through the vines.

Mal stood tall, addressing her people with a voice as

steady as steel. "Prepare yourselves. Aurora has shown her hand. She's declared war on us. It's time we fight back."

A knot of unease twisted in Phillip's gut as he stared at her. The fire in her eyes blazed bright and unrelenting. He exhaled slowly, his gaze flickering toward the distant lights of the palace—his palace—glowing like a beacon against the night sky. The place that had once been his home now felt foreign.

CHAPTER SEVENTEEN

Mal wrapped her arms tightly around herself as a shiver coursed through her. The cold was from the dampness of her clothes after their impromptu plunge into the river. She raised a hand, summoning her magic. The ground at her feet stirred, roots and tendrils bursting through the soil like eager servants. They crawled up her legs, brushing her arms, and began pulling the water from her skin. The droplets glistened on the surface of the roots before sinking into the earth like greedy sips of nourishment.

She turned to Phillip. He stood motionless, his gaze fixed on the looming castle in the distance. His broad shoulders were soaked, his tunic clinging to his chest. The roots obeyed her silent command, slithering toward him.

He didn't move. Didn't turn to her in thanks. His solemn gaze stayed fixed on the castle. His features were shadowed with sorrow, not rage.

The castle's silhouette rose against the darkening sky, jagged and foreboding. The sight ignited something hot in her chest. Anger. The thirst for retribution. Blood for blood.

"If you still think Aurora deserves your sympathy—"

"No," Phillip cut her off. "Aurora can't come back from this. Not after what she tried to do to you. For that alone, she's lost the right to my mercy."

Mal's anger didn't fade, but his words softened the sharpest edges of it. "Then what's that look for?"

"The majority of my troops are still at the borderlands. The men behind those castle walls aren't mine—they're hers. It's her army we'll face. They outnumber the forest folk."

"They do not. We have every blade of grass on our side. The trees, the roots, the very ground beneath their feet will rise up against them."

Phillip reached out, brushing a hand against her shoulder. The warmth of his touch sent a shiver through her, but not from the cold this time. "Mal, they're men like me. Some of them don't know what they're fighting for. They're just following orders."

"And if we don't fight back? If we show mercy to

those who would trample the forest and destroy everything we stand for?"

"This goes beyond taking a stand. This is war. Wars have casualties—your people... my people. This isn't what our parents planned. This isn't what either of us wanted."

There he was wrong. Many nights during the dark three years of his absence, Mal had wanted nothing but to watch the castle burn. She hadn't taken a care of who might be within the walls. She just knew Phillip wasn't within them.

"Whether we want it or not, Aurora will send those soldiers to this forest and burn it to the ground. I won't sit back and watch her destroy everything I hold dear."

The moon had barely crested over the horizon, casting a cold, gray light over the forest as Mal and Phillip stood on the ridge overlooking the clearing where Aurora's machines lay dormant. She could already see the dark shapes of soldiers marching toward the metal beasts, their swords and armor glinting in the moonlight. More were coming, their numbers stretching far back, a steady line of shadows in the distance.

"Let me try and talk to them, soldier to soldier."

"They'll listen to her first. They're loyal to her, not to you."

"They're still human," Phillip replied. "Maybe—

maybe there's a chance I can appeal to that part of them."

Mal took a breath, forcing herself to hold her tongue. Her prince was driven by a hope she no longer shared, a faith she had lost long ago. The men before them had crossed into the forest without regard, marching with machines meant to tear down the trees and flora she'd spent her life protecting. These men, they were not her allies. Even if Phillip couldn't see that, she could.

Phillip reached for her, his hand warm against her cheek. "I have to try, Mal. You rally the fae and the flora. Buy me some time."

She wanted to forbid him. Though they had their bedroom games, and Phillip never quipped about walking a step behind her—mainly so he got a look at her ass—they were always equals when in front of others. The entire forest was watching them now.

Mal's throat tightened as her heart fought against the surge of emotions that threatened to drown her. She knew him too well, knew the stubborn streak that drove him to fight battles that seemed impossible. She loved him all the more for it.

"If you die, I will kill you." Her words were laced with a desperation she couldn't hide.

Phillip's mouth curved into a grin, the kind that reached his eyes and sent warmth pooling in her chest.

He leaned down, brushing his lips over hers. "I love you, too. And I promise I'll be back. I don't break my promises to you."

"Except for the time you said you'd see me tomorrow…three years ago. And last night, when you sent a pigeon."

"No more pigeons. I'll come back for you. I'll fight by your side if I can't bring them to reason."

The weight of the moment settled over her like a cloak. Her hand itched to pull him back, to hold him close and keep him from walking into whatever danger awaited him. But she couldn't. She knew she couldn't. He was, by all rights, a king. She was queen of her own land. Their destinies were intertwined, but their paths were distinct.

Slowly, reluctantly, she released her hold on him, watching as he turned and strode down the ridge. His figure disappeared into the mist that blanketed the clearing. She stood there, rooted in place, her heart lodged painfully in her chest, her fists clenched at her sides. Every fiber of her being yearned to call him back.

She didn't. Instead, she raised her chin, squared her shoulders, and turned back to her people. They awaited her command, their eyes filled with the same grim resolve she felt in her own heart.

"Prepare yourselves. On this night, we protect our land. We fight for our home."

CHAPTER EIGHTEEN

Phillip moved through the shadows, keeping his steps light and steady. He knew these paths as well as he knew his own castle halls. They were hidden trails and shortcuts Mal had shown him long ago. They wound through the undergrowth, providing him with perfect cover. He heard the murmur of voices, the clinking of armor, and the crackling of campfires just beyond the next ridge. He drew closer to the heart of the enemy encampment, his mind already strategizing the words he would need to sway them.

Enemy.

Unfortunately, that's what they were. When he'd left to secure the borderlands, he left the castle in Aurora's hands, surrounded by her protective detail. It had never occurred to him that he was letting an adversary in so close. Though these soldiers were plenty, they weren't exactly… top tier.

Phillip easily moved past a pair of sentries. Their attention was on their dice game rather than the dark forest beyond. His path was clear, the camp's defenses laughable. He saw how he could undo their plans single-handedly: sabotage their machines, disarm their guards, or spread chaos with a false command.

The camp sprawled before him in a disorganized mess. Tents leaned precariously. Weapons were scattered about, abandoned on makeshift racks or left propped against barrels. Conversations floated through the cool night air, careless and loud. Soldiers openly discussed their orders for the tree leaves and night creatures to hear.

"They'll move at dawn," one soldier was saying, his voice carrying authority. "With the forest still dark and the creatures barely stirring, we can cut through the edge and make straight for the heart. If we're swift, the fae won't even have time to organize."

"Not that they could organize. They're plants and beasts."

There was laughter.

Phillip's hand tightened around the hilt of his sword. His stomach twisted at the callousness of the man's words. This wasn't just a campaign—it was a desecration. A betrayal of everything the forest had given their kingdom.

A blade pressed against his back, sharp enough to make the hairs on his neck rise. "Don't move."

Phillip was royalty, unused to following orders. Unless they were given by a horned fae. He turned his head slightly, enough to catch the glint of moonlight on the sword, and found the stern face of Lord Queros. The man's dark eyes narrowed, his mouth set in a grim line.

"Well, well, the prodigal prince returns. Sneaking into camps now, are we? Has the throne fallen so far?"

Phillip raised his hands slowly, feigning surrender despite the anger simmering beneath the surface. "Queros. I see you've taken to skulking about with Aurora's men rather than defending the people you swore to protect."

"That's what we're doing here, Your Highness. Expanding our borders. Ensuring humanity's survival."

Phillip's gaze flicked to the soldiers gathering behind Queros, their weapons raised but their stances uncertain. His lips curled into a faint smirk, though the pressure of the blade against his back reminded him to tread carefully. "Is that what you call destroying forests and displacing its inhabitants? My father welcomed you into these lands after you lost your king."

Aurora's soldiers exchanged glances, their grip on

their weapons loosening ever so slightly. Phillip's words cut through the veil of confidence they had tried to maintain. He saw the doubt creeping in, the uncertainty flashing in their eyes as they looked at one another, questioning, hesitating.

It was working. On them. It was one of his own citizens he had to worry about.

Lord Queros's grip tightened on his sword. "We follow the queen's command."

Technically, Aurora wasn't a queen. Not until she married Phillip. Which was never happening. But he was choosing his battles at the moment.

"I am the ruler of this land."

"The only thing ruling you is your cock. Consorting with an animal in the woods, a creature beneath your station."

So that's what this was: bigotry, pure and simple. "You won't win against the Forest Folk and their magic."

"Think your female deer will come to save you?"

Phillip heard an E instead of an A in the endearment. He vaguely remembered Mal complaining about Aurora and vowels. He focused on reining in the urge to spit out the truth—how Aurora had cursed him and betrayed both their kingdoms. But he could see the hardened faces of the men and women around him. He knew those words would fall on deaf ears tonight. So instead, he chose a different truth.

"The forest is alive. It won't be conquered, not by your machines, and certainly not by brute force. Those machines you're so confident about? They'll break down before they reach the heart of the Enchanted Forest. On foot, you'll be met by the forest folk themselves. This isn't a battlefield you can master. It's a grave you're digging for yourselves."

The soldiers shifted uneasily. Some of them, anyway. The women soldiers stood fierce and unyielding, their grips on their weapons steady, while the men glanced at one another, the slivers of doubt taking root in their eyes.

Lord Queros lowered his sword, as though Phillip was no real threat. "If you think you know so much, then act as our commander. Tell us how to defeat the forest and its creatures. How to tame this land you claim to understand so well."

Phillip held the man's gaze, his heart steadying as he allowed himself a moment of clarity, a reminder of why he was truly here. "The only way to defeat it is with love."

A heavy silence followed his words, his voice echoing in the stillness of the camp. Then, as if on cue, the men and women erupted into laughter, their voices loud and mocking, disbelief written across their faces.

Phillip's heart didn't waver, not even as their laughter filled the air. He looked out at them, and a sadness settled over him. They would never see the forest as he did, never feel its pulse, its strength. They would never understand what it meant to protect something for the love of it, to defend it not with force but with loyalty and reverence.

CHAPTER NINETEEN

*P*hillip was late. Again.

Mal clenched her fists. The bark of the tree trunk she leaned against dug into her palm as she fought the rising surge of anger—and worry—that gnawed at her. She knew Phillip wouldn't break a promise lightly. Not unless he was bound and held against his will. It had happened before. Her mind whispered that it was happening again. She tried to push the thought away, but it lingered, clinging to her like a thorn she couldn't pull free.

Mal crouched beneath the low-hanging boughs of an ancient yew. Her breath was steady. Her gaze was fixed on the distant glow of Aurora's machines. The damp, rich scent of the forest floor surrounded her, mingling with the distasteful tang of iron in the air.

Iron came from the deepest heart of the earth, where the soil and stone had grown around it, keeping it buried and hidden from the living. Life had flourished atop that buried secret, the earth sheltering its denizens from the cold, unyielding material. Sometimes, iron came not from below but above, falling from the skies when stars burned themselves out. Their celestial remains landed like intruders on the soil.

Humans had learned to shape it into weapons—alien tools to wound and destroy. The former king, wise in his understanding of both humans and Forest Folk, had banished iron from Evermore long ago, forbidding its presence in the land of magic. Aurora, with her machines and her insatiable need for control, had brought it back. She wielded it like a blight, embedding it into her mechanical monstrosities and polluting the sacred balance of the forest.

Mal's claws curled into the moss beneath her. The ancient earth pulsed beneath her palm, whispering its anger and unease. The forest stirred with her. Their rage intertwined, ready to fight back against the alien metal that sought to poison their sanctuary. Mal couldn't wait any longer.

"Begin the strike."

Dryads marched forward, calling up the roots of their ancestors. Tree roots shot up from the ground like writhing serpents, twisting around steel beams, prying open metal plates with relentless strength. The vines crept into the machinery, snaking through gears and circuits, spreading like veins under their guidance. The screech of tearing metal filled the air, mingling with the furious whirs and clanks of the sabotaged machines.

That was the first offensive. Had the humans not learned from their earlier encounter with Mal, the battle would have been over, the war won. Unfortunately, these weren't the dumbest of the lot.

A flank of soldiers moved in, weapons raised. Sprites darted through the trees, leaving trails of shimmering dust in their wake as they got into position. On the ground, the humans moved with confidence, expecting nothing more than resistance from the dryads and the trees. What they didn't expect were the animals.

From the underbrush came the crashing sound as deer charged forward, their antlers lowered like natural lances. Bears emerged next, their powerful forms barreling through the human ranks with roars that sent chills down even the bravest spines. Wolves wove in and out of the fray, their sharp teeth and cunning eyes glinting as they drove the humans into disarray. Birds dived from above, their talons sharp as they clawed at helmets and unprotected faces. Even the smallest creatures played their part. Raccoons darted in to pull weapons from distracted hands, while squirrels leapt onto shoulders, clawing and biting with surprising ferocity.

Chaos erupted among the humans. Their tight formation unraveled in the face of the forest's fury. Shouts of panic rang out. Swords clattered to the ground as men and women scrambled to defend themselves from the onslaught. It was then that the sprites and fairies struck.

Magic rippled through the air, unseen threads that coiled around wrists and ankles, binding the humans in place. Glittering nets of enchanted light descended upon clusters of soldiers, immobilizing them with unbreakable bonds. One by one, the humans fell to the ground, disarmed and helpless, as the fae encircled them.

Mal watched from the edge of the clearing. She felt no pity for the intruders, only a grim satisfaction as the forest claimed its justice. These humans had marched into her domain, swords drawn, without understanding that the land itself would rise against them. Victory was imminent. Yet her mind kept drifting, scanning the tree line, searching.

Where the hell was he?

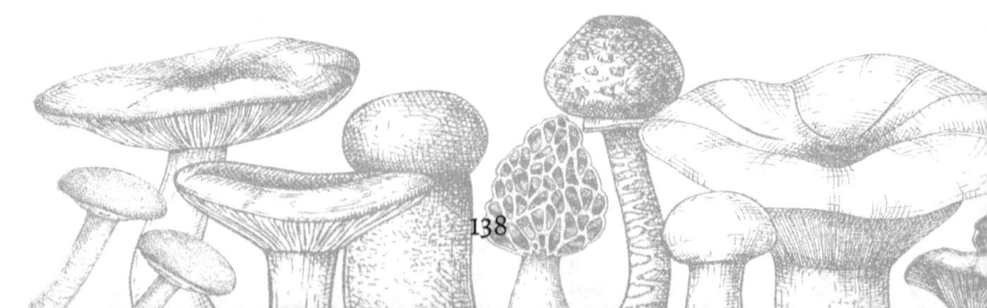

CHAPTER TWENTY

*P*hillip tasted the stale air in the army tent. It was thick with the scent of sweat and smoke. His wrists were bound tightly behind him. The skin chafed against the coarse rope. The raw flesh stung with every shift. The ache in his shoulders grew sharper. But it was the sounds outside that held his focus.

Shouts of alarm. The thunderous crash of something heavy falling. The eerie howl of wolves blending with human screams. He caught the sharp, splintering crack of trees—a sound that normally would have filled him with dread—but this time, he recognized it for what it was. The forest was fighting back.

His heart swelled with pride. Mal had done it. She'd rallied the forest folk, the creatures, and the land

139

itself to rise against their enemies. He could see her in his mind's eye, fierce and unyielding, the very embodiment of nature's wrath and power. This was the woman he loved—unstoppable, vicious, and victorious.

With the pride came an ache, a heavy sadness settling in his chest. He knew too well the cost of such battles. Every triumphant roar of the forest was mirrored by the cries of those who fell—human and fae alike. Lives were being lost, wounds inflicted, and even more division between his people and hers was likely being sown.

A quiet rustle pulled him from his thoughts, and he glanced up. His guard—a young soldier with a weary face, his eyes cast down—stood by the tent's flap. He cast a nervous glance outside. Shadows flickered as torches lit up the surrounding darkness.

"Not going well out there?"

The young man shifted, caught off guard. Something hesitant flickered in his eyes. "My neighbor's son is a fae. That boy, he... he always helps my mother with her garden, especially her herb garden. If it wasn't for him, I'd be eating tasteless foods. I was just wondering if he was out there… fighting."

"There shouldn't be sides, not when we are neighbors."

"I agree." His words were almost a whisper.

Phillip seized the chance. "Then help me. Untie me, and we'll find a way to make this right."

The young man's gaze flickered with uncertainty, but he took a step forward. His hands reached for the knots. Phillip held his breath, waiting, willing the guard's resolve to hold.

The tent flap whipped open. His chances were lost. It would be Lord Queros come to end him. Or worse, take him back to Aurora as a bargaining chip.

Mal strode in, her presence commanding and fierce. She was drenched in forest magic, her dark eyes alight with determination, and for a moment, he forgot every thing but the sight of her.

"You're late."

"I was on my way." Phillip grinned, leaning into her glare. "Made a new friend in the meantime."

The guard gulped when Mal turned a hard look on him. It was her murderous look. The one that had made Phillip fall in love with her. Surprisingly, it didn't have the same effect with other males. Their loss.

The young man took a step back. His hands dropped from Phillip's bonds as he silently conceded. He may have wet his pants a little, but Phillip was too decent to point that out.

With a snap of her fingers, Mal handled the knots that bound him. The ropes, which were made of hemp, fell away with a soft thud to the ground. His fingers tingled with returning circulation, but he reached for her.

The warmth of her skin, her wild, earthy scent, filled his senses like the forest itself had come alive within her. He leaned in, pressing his lips to hers. The kiss tasted of her magic, of rain-drenched soil and sun-warmed leaves. A flood of life and relief stole his breath, melding both their sighs of relief into a single exhale.

"Seems you've got things well in hand." Phillip rested his forehead against Mal's.

"Not if you keep needing rescuing."

Phillip chuckled softly, the sound more relief than humor. Mal wasn't done. She tugged him closer for another kiss. This one was slower, deeper, as if reclaiming a piece of him that had been missing for years. He let her strength seep into him like a balm over old wounds.

"The machines are down. The earth is devouring them as we speak. The leadership, including Lord Queros, has surrendered."

Relief surged through Phillip, so potent it nearly buckled his knees. He exhaled shakily, his shoulders sagging as the tension began to drain from him. "It's over."

"No, not yet."

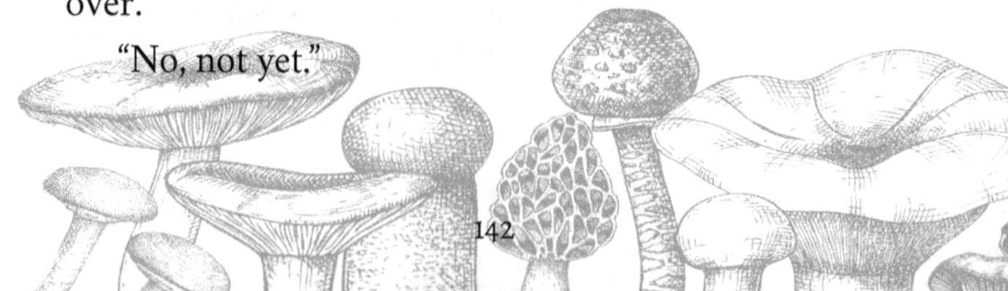

Mal's next words hit like a blow. Her voice, when she spoke, was dark, cold and resolute.

"Now to the castle to kill the princess."

For the first time since the fighting began, Phillip wasn't sure they wanted the same victory. He stepped back, searching his beloved's face for any hint of hesitation.

Mal's expression was as unyielding as stone. No, not stone. Iron.

<h1 style="text-align:center">CHAPTER TWENTY-ONE</h1>

"**M**al, listen to me. Killing Aurora won't solve this."

"Won't solve it?"

Aurora's machines lay strewn like broken toys along the path. Their metal gleamed in the dappled light. Even now, even with Phillip at her side trying to plead reason, Mal couldn't shake the urge to tear through every last piece of machinery that dared to invade her land. The only solution to this was keeping that pritch far, far away from her forests. And if she wouldn't leave them in peace, she was dead.

Mal so hope Aurora resisted.

Phillip stepped around a twisted heap of gears and grabbed her hand, forcing her to stop. "Mal, not everyone in the realm wants this. Not every human would stand by while the forest burns."

"What about her soldiers? Were they just following orders?"

As if on cue, a blur of movement caught Mal's attention. The young sprite she'd saved only days before raced toward an injured human. There was a makeshift blade in her hand. The sprite's face twisted with a dangerous resolve that no child's face should carry. She landed on the soldier's chest, blade glinting in the moonlight.

"Stop!"

Mal's voice cut through the air, and the sprite froze. A cherubic face looked up with wide, fierce eyes. Mal closed the distance between them, heart pounding as she knelt before the girl.

"Put it down."

"He hurt the forest." The sprite's was voice laced with a bitterness that twisted Mal's heart. "He hurt our kind."

Mal saw her own younger self mirrored in the child's fierce, wild eyes. Her anger was unchecked and untempered. If the sprite wasn't careful, that fire would twist and scar. It had gnawed at Mal for so long, warping her, hardening her heart. Phillip had been the one to soften it, to show her that strength didn't have to come from fury. But Phillip was a rare light in this world. This child—she didn't have a Phillip to save her from the darkness gnawing at her heart.

"Yes, he did." Mal placed her hand over the sprite's, gently pressing until her grip slackened, guiding her to let the blade drop. It fell with a hollow clink against the mossy ground, a fragile thing, so brittle compared to the enormity of the forest around them.

Mal looked to Phillip, hoping he'd offer some of his boundless, infuriating optimism. He only nodded, his gaze soft, but he left her to find the words herself. Mal took a breath, feeling the weight of the sprite's anger settle in her chest.

"I know what it's like to carry anger so big it feels like it could tear the world apart. I know what it's like to see hurt and think that the only answer is more hurt. If we let that anger grow, it will twist us. It doesn't matter if we think we're in the right. We don't fight to destroy, do we? We fight to protect. The forest needs us whole. Strong, but not consumed."

The sprite looked down at the human. The man had long since slipped into unconsciousness. He was no threat. "What if they come back?"

Mal didn't have an answer to that. Luckily, Phillip did.

"We will welcome them back."

Both Mal and the sprite looked at him with disbelieving eyes.

"But we won't let them pass if they have hatred in their hearts. The forest and the castle will no longer be open to hateful hearts." Phillip got down to the sprite's level. "Do you have hatred in your heart?"

The sprite twisted her lips. The answer wasn't yet no, but the child did open her hand and accepted Phillip's offer of help to her feet.

"These soldiers were fighting for a crown, for a single person," Phillip continued, his voice carrying to the Forest Folk who'd gathered, to the tree limbs that bowed to listen. "We fight for each other. For every tree, every stream, every creature that needs us. For those we love. It's harder, yes, but strength tempered by love is the only thing that keeps the forest truly alive."

Phillip kept the sprite's hand in his. He reached out with his other to Mal. She inhaled deeply. As she let the breath out, she twined her fingers with his.

By the roots, the love of her life was such a sap.

"Life is precious, every life. Your people, mine. We fight to protect, not to destroy."

The sprite's fierce expression crumpled. She nodded slowly, eyes wet as she glanced at the human lying helpless on the ground. When she turned and disappeared into the trees, Mal looked at Phillip, a quiet resignation replacing the earlier anger in her gaze.

"You win," she huffed. "I'll talk to Aurora. But don't ask me to compromise more than that. I won't give up my land, and I certainly won't give you up. If she makes a play for you, I will chop off her hair."

Phillip grinned down at her with a smile, like a cat who found the cream. "I can accept those terms."

CHAPTER TWENTY-TWO

Storming the castle wasn't going as Phillip planned. The number one reason was that people were streaming out of the castle instead of hunkering down inside and defending it. Phillip tightened his grip on Mal's hand as they stepped into the courtyard. The cries of the fleeing crowd rang in his ears. It was Phillip's small regiment of soldiers who had accompanied him back that were guiding the people out, helping them as they stumbled over broken stones and splintered wood.

Aurora's soldiers? Nowhere in sight. They'd abandoned their posts, scattered like leaves in a storm. Many of them were already beyond the castle walls in the hands of the Forest Folks.

"What's her play?" Mal's skeptical gaze scanned the chaos. "This feels too easy."

Phillip nodded. A heavy sense of foreboding settled over him as they reached the grand archway leading into the castle. The halls beyond were empty, devoid of the guards that should have lined every entrance. The usual clatter of armor and footsteps was replaced by an eerie silence, broken only by the distant sound of crumbling stone and the occasional cry of a wounded soul.

He'd known Aurora since she was a child, had watched her grow from a naïve princess into something far more dangerous. And yet, even realizing her ruthlessness, he hadn't expected her to abandon their people in such a way. The Aurora he'd once known wouldn't have left her own soldiers to fend for themselves. The woman they were about to confront was clearly a stranger to him.

The castle doors opened, and they made their way into the throne room. The dim light cast long, foreboding shadows across the room's expanse. There, seated on his father's throne, was Aurora. Her back was straight, her expression poised, as if this were nothing more than a routine court meeting.

Beside her perched Ariel. The sea princess's eyes glimmered with a cold, unsettling mirth. Ariel couldn't speak. She'd been born without a voice box. But that had never stopped her and Rory from communicating on their visits. The sea fairy's hands moved in subtle gestures, a silent language only Aurora seemed to understand.

Mal's voice cut through the silence. "I thought you hated fae. Yet here you are, cozying up to the sea folk."

Aurora's eyes flicked toward them, a slow, amused smile creeping onto her lips as her gaze landed on Mal. She lifted Ariel's hand, running her fingers over it in a possessive gesture. "Oh, I've never hated fae. Except the ones who thought they could steal my future and twist it into something that suited them."

"Aurora." Phillip stepped forward, his tone measured, still trying for diplomacy. "You know I loved Maleficent long before you were even born. I told you that."

"You misunderstand, Phillip. You were never my future. The idea of being another pawn in someone else's game—whether it was my father's or yours—was something I vowed to shatter."

Aurora turned back to Mal, her gaze coldly triumphant. "There was a prophecy about me, you know. It was foretold that a fairy's curse would end my life. Death by spindle, isn't that tragic? So my father, the dutiful king, had every spinning wheel in the kingdom destroyed."

Phillip only vaguely remembered this story. His father had told him of his betrothed's curse when he'd brought the spindle into the tower of forbidden objects. That was the day that he'd stolen his first kiss from Mal. So the details had always been a little hazy.

"Imagine my surprise when I found my murder weapon in my fiancé's tower."

"You think I would've hurt you?"

"Hurt me, Phillip? No. Ignore me. Overlook me. Use me as a pawn while you rutted with a deer out in the fields."

Phillip felt a chill go through him. This was the Aurora he'd sensed lurking beneath her polite smiles and demure glances, a woman willing to destroy anyone in her path. "What do you want, Aurora?"

Aurora's lips twitched in a smile that held no remorse. "All I want is to be free, to choose my path, to love who I will."

"Then go and do that. No one's stopping you."

Mal's claws bit into Phillip's wrist as though she wanted to step forward.

Phillip tucked her closer to his side. They were almost out of this with no more bloodshed. "Your army has fallen. It's over. You've lost."

Aurora laughed, a sound as cold as it was dismissive. "That was my father's army." She glanced at Ariel, who met her gaze with a soft, adoring smile. "I'm using my girlfriend's forces now."

The doors swung open. A line of mermen entered, tridents gleaming in their hands. Iron tridents.

Mal's grip went weak in his hand as the poisonous metal cast its presence over the room. Her skin paled, her breath catching as the poison sapped her strength. Phillip stepped in front of her, shielding her as best as he could from the advancing soldiers.

"Aurora, whatever twisted version of freedom you seek, it doesn't have to come through bloodshed."

Aurora's voice was now stripped of any sweetness. "It's too late for compromises, Phillip. I am not a pawn, and I will not share this world with anyone who thinks they can put me to bed to sleepwalk through life." Her gaze flickered to Mal with a look of utter contempt.

Ariel signaled to the mermen. The soldiers raised their tridents, points trained on Phillip and Mal. Rage built within Phillip as he realized they were vastly outnumbered and Mal was weakening fast.

CHAPTER TWENTY-THREE

The mermen lunged toward Mal. Phillip released her hand to raise his sword. Mal raised her hands. Her magic faltered.

The sting of iron filled the air. Its bite seeped into her like venom, dulling her magic and slowing her movements. She was surrounded by stone—no soil, no roots to draw from. The castle was barren of life.

The walls were adorned with artwork. There were ornate tapestries depicting fields of wildflowers and groves of ancient trees. The drawings were pretty but did her no good.

Her eyes landed on the decorative vases arranged near the dais. The flowers inside were brittle and dry. The best they would do was crumble to dust at contact.

And then she felt it.

Beneath the stone floor, deep in the cracks where light never touched, she sensed moss clinging to life, fed by the faintest moisture. Beyond the walls, ivy crept along the castle's outer facade, its tendrils slowly finding their way into forgotten crevices. It wasn't much, but it was something.

Mal extended her hand toward the floor. Her magic was like a whisper at first. The moss responded, its tendrils unfurling with startling speed, snaking through the cracks and creeping toward the room. The ivy answered her call, its delicate tendrils bursting through the window frames, curling inward with surprising strength.

The first merman advanced, his trident flashing. Mal ducked low, narrowly avoiding the strike, and thrust her hand forward. Vines erupted into the room, wrapping around his legs and yanking him off balance. He hit the ground with a crash, his trident clattering out of reach.

Phillip's blade flashed in the torchlight as he engaged another merman. Their weapons clashed with a deafening clang. Phillip's sword sliced through the air with precision, fending off each trident strike that came his way. The mermen were strong, well-trained, and relentless, but Mal and Phillip moved as a single force.

From the throne, Aurora and Ariel watched with a

twisted sort of glee, lazily picking at a platter of fruit and small cakes as if the battle were nothing more than a passing amusement.

Mal's anger flared. She forced herself to stay focused, her mind sharp even as the iron weighed her down.

She reached deeper into the room. Her magic latched on to the wooden beams overhead, calling to the ancient timber. It groaned, a low, ominous creak that filled the chamber. The mermen paused, their fish-like eyes flicking upward. With a flick of her wrist, a beam splintered free, crashing down onto two of them, knocking them unconscious.

The furniture answered next. A heavy chair slid across the floor. It rammed into a merman and pinned him against the wall. A table's legs twisted unnaturally, tripping another as he tried to retreat. Phillip stood over the last fallen merman, breathing heavily, a smudge of blood on his cheek.

"Why," Aurora sneered, her voice dripping with venom, "won't you just die and leave me in peace?"

Phillip sheathed his sword. "You're in my castle, Aurora. I'm giving you a chance to leave now and go home. There's no need for any more of this."

"This is my home now, Phillip. I already redecorated. Or didn't you notice the new draperies?"

Ariel rose from her seat, her movements fluid and

graceful, like waves rolling across the sea. She opened her mouth and made a hissing sound. The hisses were words. Unintelligible words that Mal couldn't understand.

But Phillip could.

His expression shifted. His eyes grew vacant. His movements became mechanical as he turned toward her.

"Phillip…?"

The eyes that were always warm eyes stared through her, empty and cold.

His fist swung toward her, catching her off guard. She dodged just in time. His knuckles grazed her cheek. Mal backed up, disbelief mingling with the pain.

This was Phillip, her Phillip. And yet he was gone, as though he was caught under a siren's call. Mal had heard stories of such creatures, but she'd always thought they were myths.

"Phillip, snap out of it. I don't want to hurt you."

He didn't respond. Instead, he lunged at her again with the same vacant, hollow stare. Each strike he threw was jerky, like a puppet being controlled by invisible strings.

"Phillip!" she cried, ducking another strike. "Fight it—please, you're stronger than this."

His movements faltered. A flicker of recognition

flashed in his eyes. Ariel's voice hissed through the air again, the haunting melody sealing her hold on him.

"You love me," cried Mal.

"I do love you." He threw another punch.

"You promised you'd never hurt me."

"Am I hurting you, Mal?"

"Yes!"

Mal steeled herself, her heart aching as she made her choice. With a deft move, she ducked beneath his next strike and yanked the sword from its sheath. The weight of the blade in her hands was a reminder of everything they stood to lose.

She took a step back, her gaze locking with his for what felt like a lifetime.

"I love you," she said, her voice steady even as her heart fractured. "You're my reason for living."

Phillip lunged toward her. Mal's arm snapped forward. The blade whistled through the air, aimed not at him, but past him. It struck true.

A piercing scream ripped through the throne room as the sword buried itself in the throne. From the blade fell a curtain of blond hair… and the remnants of Aurora's ear.

Ariel's haunting melody broke into a discordant shriek as her control shattered. Aurora's hands cupped what was left of her ear.

Phillip staggered as the siren's hold released its grasp. His eyes cleared, the vacancy replaced with horror as he took in the scene before him. "Mal..." he croaked, his voice raw.

"I told you I'd take her hair if she made a play for you."

CHAPTER TWENTY-FOUR

*P*hillip's vision sharpened as he blinked out of Ariel's spell. The hazy fog of her siren call lifted like a heavy weight from his mind as Aurora's blond locks floated to the ground with red tints at their edges. He didn't feel the slightest hint of irritation at Mal. Didn't feel an ounce of sorrow for Rory. She'd been warned. What made him see past the red of Aurora's blood were the bruises on Mal.

They were from his own hands. Guilt hit him. The sensation wrenched his heart in ways he hadn't known it could twist.

"Mal…"

She held up a hand, cutting him off with a shake of her head. Her head wasn't the only thing shaking. A deep, unsettling rumble rolled through the walls, like a low growl from the very bones of the castle.

It was Ariel. The sea fairy's piercing wails filled the air. The awful sounds shook the stone foundations around them. Outside the tall windows, water rose unnaturally high. Waves thrashed like enraged beasts as they crashed toward the castle walls.

"We have to get everyone out." Phillip pulled Mal to him.

With a final glance toward the throne room, where Ariel and Aurora were on the floor like broken statues amidst the chaos they had unleashed, Phillip turned away. Together, he and Mal raced down the corridors, their hands intertwined, calling out to the soldiers, servants, and forest folk alike.

Footsteps thundered. Voices cried out. The distant roar of waves crashed through the lower levels of the castle.

"If we raise the gates, we'll flood the village and castle," said one of the guards who helped a servant to her feet.

"It's the only way to not kill everyone," said Phillip. "We go to the forests."

"The Forest Folk will kill us," insisted the guard.

"They will not," said Mal. "That is if your heart is open."

The guard looked at her with a screwed-up expression, as though he didn't understand her words. Mal lifted a brow at Phillip. He wanted to tell her that she didn't sell the philosophy correctly. But they had more pressing matters to attend to—namely the imminent flood.

Mal called out orders to the forest folk, leading them toward safer paths. Phillip shouted commands to his people, ensuring they stayed clear of the rising water.

They moved as a team, shifting to support those around them. Mal helped an elderly man who'd fallen behind. She lifted him up with a gentleness he knew only a few ever saw from her. He felt his heart tighten, his chest swelling with an aching pride and a fierce, protective love.

Finally, they reached the forests. The last group of people breached the sacred tree circle in the cloak of the night. Just as the final stragglers stumbled to safety, a monstrous wave crashed against the stone walls of the keep, sending a tremor through the ground.

Phillip watched his home—his legacy—being swallowed by the relentless tide. The water surged through the windows, flooding the great halls and snuffing out the torches that had once cast such proud light across the castle grounds. The golden tapestries, the portraits of his ancestors, the legacy of his family—it was all disappearing, one wave at a time.

"It's… it's gone."

Mal's hand tightened in his, pulling him back from the despair that threatened to swallow him too. He turned, meeting her gaze. Her eyes were dark, fierce, yet filled with a steady reassurance that he didn't have to face this alone.

"You still have your people," she said.

"He has your people too," said Doran.

Around him, the dryads and sprites and other fae all gave their acquiescence.

Mal turned so that all could see and hear her. "We've all suffered loss here on this day. Loss of family, loss of land. But we will rebuild. Together."

Phillip turned, giving the castle, his legacy, his back. He pulled his longtime love and future wife into his arms and looked out at the folk and people looking back at the two of them for guidance. He took a slow, steadying breath.

The cool night air filled his lungs. He allowed himself to let go of the past, of the expectations and burdens he'd carried for so long. The castle was gone, yes. But the people, his people and hers, were still here, standing beside him.

Phillip felt a wave of gratitude for Mal, for the strength she lent him in his weakest moments. For the love she showed him, both in private and out in the open. He loved his people, but he lived for this woman.

CHAPTER TWENTY-FIVE

Mal stirred, her senses coming alive in a warm, gentle haze. Phillip's arm was draped over her, solid and comforting, his body a shield against the chill of the morning. His steady breath was against her hair. The heat of his chest rested against her back. She let herself stay there, nestled in the quiet. Wrapped in the illusion that last night had been some strange dream. That the chaos, the fighting, the tidal wave, and the crumbling of the castle walls had been nothing more than a story her mind had conjured up.

But dreams always gave way to daylight. She opened her eyes and looked out the window of her cabin. The remnants of that shattered reality lay just beyond the forest. The broken stones of the castle, its once-majestic walls, were all reduced to jagged remnants.

The towers were now hollow against the dawn sky. Smoke rose from the ruins, faint wisps twisting into the air. The scattered remains of what had once been Phillip's home loomed over them.

Phillip shifted beside her, his arm tightening as he stirred. His hand brushed along her shoulder. His touch was instinctively protective, even in his half-asleep state. The urge to reach out, to reassure herself that he was real, was overwhelming.

Beyond the boundaries of the forest, tents had been erected in hastily cleared patches of land, forming clusters of makeshift shelters. Humans, displaced from their homes, milled about in the early light, their faces etched with weariness and loss. Outside her bedroom window, she heard snippets of frustrated murmurs. The faint sounds of disputes broke out over cramped space and lost belongings. The human world was no longer one of order and rigid structure, but of survival.

Phillip's hand moved to her cheek, brushing a stray lock of hair back as his eyes met hers. "You're awake." His voice was rough with sleep yet filled with a quiet joy she hadn't seen in so long. "I thought I might have dreamed you."

"You'd better believe I'm real. Otherwise, there's something else holding your cock."

He chuckled softly, a low, comforting sound that

filled the remaining cracks within her. "Whatever has a hold on me, I never want it to let go."

Mal tightened her hold on him. A happy gasp escaped the wide smile on his mouth. "Good," she purred. "Because I'm never letting go."

She caressed her prince until he spilled in her hand. Before his spend cooled in her palm, he had her on her back, her knees resting against his shoulders. His tongue did beautifully wicked things to her beneath the sheets until she begged him for mercy.

He gave her none.

His cock hard once more, he prowled up her body and thrust into her heat. At first fast and hard. Then slow and languorous. The urgency to reach another peak was far from their minds.

They stayed like that, suspended in a moment of peace, until a rustling outside drew their attention. A young fae child, her wings tattered but her eyes bright, walked past the cabin window. She carried a small bundle of food. In her wake followed a human boy, perhaps a year or two younger, who trailed her with besotted eyes, watching her wings with a mixture of awe and trepidation.

It was strange, this new world where fae and humans existed side by side. Where boundaries that had once seemed unbreachable had begun to blur.

Phillip watched the children. His expression shifted

into something contemplative. "We have work ahead of us."

"We should probably start by closing the curtains."

He chuckled, slowly pulling out of her. He rose from the bed and walked to the window, gloriously naked. His gaze lifted to the castle in the distance. "The castle, the lands… it all has to be rebuilt."

They had lost much, more than either of them could put into words. The castle had fallen, but the forest had also suffered. Mal wanted to believe it was possible. She wanted to believe that the forest folk and humans could rebuild something new. But the path ahead was anything but clear. Still, there was one truth louder than the tidal wave that had nearly taken them out.

"We're stronger together than we ever were apart."

Phillip shut the curtains and returned to bed. He gathered Mal into his arms and held her close. Just this simple touch and she felt like she could single-handedly rebuild their entire world by herself. But she wouldn't have to do it alone. She had him.

"Aurora and Ariel may have escaped."

That soured Mal's mood. If Phillip hadn't already given her three orgasms, she would've been upset about him bringing up his ex while they were naked. "We'll be ready for them if they return.

"I don't think they'll return."

Mal didn't care one way or another. If Aurora was

still alive, and if she was dumb enough to mount a second attack, Mal would aim the next blow lower, right at her heart.

"They may have shattered what our parents tried to build," Phillip was saying. "But we'll create something even stronger. This time… we'll do it our way."

His fingers curled around hers, entwining their hands. The traces of last night's destruction wouldn't stay hidden behind the curtains for long. As they lay together, there was an undeniable sense of promise in the air—a promise of rebuilding, of mending what had been torn apart by a cursed spindle.

EPILOGUE

The great coral doors of King Triton's court loomed before Ursula like a whale's mouth waiting to devour her whole. She entered with her proud head cast down as would a guppy seeking castoffs in the wake of a human's ship. It was demeaning, but she had very few choices these days. So she pressed forward. If there was one thing she could never be accused of, it was lacking audacity.

At her first opportunity, she broke away from the school of simpering merpeople and sought her own path. Ursula glided forward, her dark figure casting elongated shadows across the shimmering floor. She knew these halls like they were her own home because once upon a time, they had been.

The once-familiar corridors seemed smaller now,

shrunken by time and her exile. Each twist and turn of the castle whispered memories she would rather forget. A snide comment from her father here, a rebuke from Triton there. The laughter of her cousins echoing in a chamber she had never quite belonged to.

Still, she swam deeper until the voices of the court grew faint. Ursula found herself before a door she hadn't seen in years. Her fingers brushed against its coral frame, and her lips curled into a sneer.

This room had once been hers.

She eased the door open, slipping inside. The interior was unrecognizable. Gone were her elegant seashell furnishings and maps of the ocean floor. Instead, the space was cluttered, overflowing with an assortment of mismatched objects. Forks and candlesticks hung from seaweed strands like decorations. Rusted trinkets and chipped porcelain plates lined the walls.

Ursula's sneer deepened as she took it all in. The youngest princess, Ariel, had turned this room into an ode to her ridiculous obsession with the human world. The air breathers. Ariel's fascination with their kind bordered on sickness, as far as Ursula was concerned. What value could these crude, corroded baubles possibly hold?

She swam past a pile of tarnished silverware and stopped at a vanity adorned with pearls and aquamarine. Her gaze locked on a small chest half-buried beneath a tangle of nets. Flipping it open, Ursula smiled. Inside was a collection of gleaming jewels—emeralds, sapphires, rubies, all shimmering like captured starlight.

Her fingers lingered on a particularly large sapphire. This stone had belonged to their grandmother. It had been passed down to Ursula, but Triton hadn't allowed her to take it with her when he'd banished her. She tightened her grip and tucked it away with the rest.

This wasn't thievery. Not that Ursula had a problem with taking anything from the royal family. These jewels were her birthright. She emptied the chest of jewels and slipped them into her cloak. With one last glance at the chaotic space, she slipped back into the hallway.

A shadow passed over the corridor ahead. Ursula froze, shrinking into the corner as a patrol of guards approached. One of them paused, sniffing the water.

"Did you hear something?"

The other guard yawned. "Probably just a crab."

Ursula rolled her eyes. She could almost pity her brother for ruling over such imbeciles. Almost.

The guards lumbered past, and Ursula resumed her escape, but she paused when she turned the next corner. There, floating at the far end of the hall, was Triton himself.

Her big brother was the only one who could see through her illusions. No matter how carefully she masked her appearance, her brother's piercing eyes would always find her.

He was distracted now. He gripped his golden trident in one hand. His brow furrowed as he spoke to one of his advisors.

"She's still missing?"

"Yes, Your Majesty."

"I don't understand why the princess keeps disappearing," said a lady's maid whom Ursula somewhat recognized. The woman had been in attendance to her when she was the jewel of the crown.

"It's likely bridal nerves," suggested the advisor. "Her betrothed arrives tomorrow."

Betrothed? So big brother had gone and gotten his last daughter on a hook. Ursula wondered with which ocean.

"This alliance between the King of Marinelle," barked her brother.

Marinelle? That was no ocean. That was land; a land of humans.

"Send out a search party. We cannot afford a delay. My daughter must meet Prince Eric at the docks tomorrow morning, or the trading agreement could collapse. This alliance is vital to the kingdom. She must be present. Find her!"

Poor, precious Ariel. So adored, so sheltered—and so utterly incapable of handling the pressures of royal life.

Ursula had tried to warn her father. She'd told him that Triton's guppies didn't have the mettle to rule. And what had she gotten for her troubles? Passed over by her father and banished by her brother.

Well, this was them all getting their just desserts.

"Princess Ariel?"

Ursula froze for half a heartbeat before her lips curled into an amused grin. The guard's mistake was delicious. She and Ariel shared the same red hair and sharp features. The resemblance had always been uncanny—a source of bitterness during her years in the court.

The guard frowned, confusion creeping into his gaze as he looked closer. "Wait... you're not—"

Before he could finish, Ursula straightened, her voice taking on a low, hypnotic hum. "You saw nothing," she said, her words rippling through the water, melodic and irresistible. "You will not go out to look for the princess. You will go and get drunk instead. Do you understand?"

The guard's expression went slack, his earlier suspicion dissolving under the weight of her siren's song. "Get... drunk."

Ursula smiled, her teeth glinting in the dim light. "Good boy. Now off you go."

The guard swam past her, dazed but determined, his earlier mistake already forgotten.

Ursula lingered in the corridor, her mind alight with a new idea. For too long, she'd been reduced to sneaking around the kingdom that should've been hers. She'd been the one that had to go around hiding who she was to survive.

That would all stop. Not tonight. Tonight, she would sneak into Marinelle and meet the human prince face to face. It would be her face that he looked upon, but it would be Ariel's name that she gave him.

She flexed her fingers, power crackling faintly in the water around her. Ariel was missing, and Triton was desperate. The prince was expecting a wide-eyed, innocent princess—but what he'd get was someone far more cunning.

With a dark laugh, Ursula slipped into the depths, her plan fully formed. By the time she surfaced, she would no longer be the outcast sister. She would be married to the prince and return to her throne as queen.

Want to read Ursula and Eric's story?

Grab your copy of *Wicked Song*
Book Two in the Wicked Evermore series.

ABOUT INES JOHNSON

Lover of fairytales, folklore, and mythology, Ines Johnson spends her days reimagining the stories of old in a modern world. She writes books where damsels cause the distress, princesses wield swords, and moms save the world.

If you liked Ines' Beast then you'll love her Vampires and Dragons. To find out more just visit https://ineswrites.com/ReaderGroup

Want More FANTASY ROMANCE by INES JOHNSON?

Wicked Evermore
Wicked Beauty
Wicked Song
Wicked Chill

The Lunaterra Chronicles

The Beastly Crown
The Beautiful Blade

Immortal Vices and Virtues
Forbid Me
Reveal Me